"Why didn't you tell me all this in London?"

"Would you have believed me?" Badyr asked. "Since you still regard me as a wicked, lascivious villain."

"Well, I..." Leonie blushed, stunned by the intimate warmth and charm of Badyr's smile.

"I'm still awaiting your answer," he murmured. "Are you willing to help me develop my country? Or do you feel it's a task beyond your mental and physical capabilities?"

"No, of course it isn't!" she protested. "But there's so much to discuss...and I haven't exactly agreed to anything."

"Oh, yes you have and I'm quite confident that you will perform the services I require to perfection." With a low husky laugh he drew her into their bedroom, closing the door. "Just as certain as I am that you will perfectly perform the, er, service I require tonight!"

MARY LYONS is happily married to an Essex farmer, has two children and lives in an old Victorian rectory. Life is peaceful—unlike her earlier years when she worked as a radio announcer, reviewed books and even ran for Parliament in a London dockland area. She still loves a little excitement and combines romance with action and suspense in her books whenever possible.

Books by Mary Lyons

These books may be available at your local bookseller.

Don't miss any of our special offers. Write to us at the following address for information on our newest releases.

Harlequin Reader Service
901 Fuhrmann Blvd., P.O. Box 1397, Buffalo, NY 14240
Canadian address: P.O. Box 603,
Fort Erie, Ont. L2A 9Z9

MARY LYONS

escape from the harem

Harlequin Books

TORONTO • NEW YORK • LONDON
AMSTERDAM • PARIS • SYDNEY • HAMBURG
STOCKHOLM • ATHENS • TOKYO • MILAN

Harlequin Presents first edition December 1986
ISBN 0-373-10938-5

Original hardcover edition published in 1986
by Mills & Boon Limited

CHAPTER ONE

'Oh Leonie, honey, I really can't decide...' Mrs Kaminsky gave a helpless shrug as she looked around the large, draughty warehouse. 'I never imagined—I mean, honest to God, honey,' she added plaintively, 'I've never seen so many damn rugs in all my born days!'

'Yes, it can be confusing.' Leonie gave the petite American woman a brief, sympathetic smile before turning to consult some papers on a clipboard, which rested on a pile of carpets beside her tall figure.

A shaft of autumn sunlight streaming down from the high, dusty window illuminated the fiery glow of her reddish-gold, long curly hair, piled loosely up in a knot on top of her head. Her wide sapphire-blue eyes, heavily fringed with dark feathery eyelashes, gazed pensively at the notes she had made earlier in the day. This was the third warehouse that she and Mrs Kaminsky had visited that morning, and they were getting nowhere. Her client was obviously wilting at the knees, and becoming increasingly bewildered by the enormous variety of rugs and carpets available on display.

'My husband told me that London is the centre of the world market for Oriental rugs and carpets, but he never said anything about having to trudge around all these nasty old buildings,' Mrs Kaminsky moaned, clutching her pale mink coat about her slim figure. 'It sure seems a weird way to do business—and mighty tough on the feet!' she added wearily, seating herself on a pile of glowing silk Isfahan carpets.

Leonie smiled patiently, before attempting to explain the position yet again. 'It's my task, as an Oriental

carpet broker, to take you around the various
warehouses and help you to buy the best and most
suitable rug at the keenest price. The stock you see here
has come from all quarters of the globe, and because
my firm, Kashan's, doesn't have expensive store
premises to maintain, and only charge a small buying
commission, you get a completely unbiased opinion on
the merchandise for sale. That means that you save a *lot*
of money and we personally guarantee the quality of
the item you choose.'

The American woman gave a heavy sigh. 'Okay,
honey, I get the point—dollarwise. But why can't I just
have a few rugs sent to the hotel? That way I could take
my time deciding which one I want?'

'I know it's not an ideal situation,' Leonie agreed.
'But everything you see here is being held under a
customs and excise bond. Which means that when
you've picked a rug you like, we can ship it straight
over to your home in Palm Springs, and thus avoid you
having to pay customs duty—a sum which would have
to be charged if the rug left this warehouse.'

'I guess you're right, but I'm feeling ab-sol-lutely
pooped—and in no shape to traipse around any more
of these damn, dusty buildings!'

'I'm sure we'll find just what you're looking for,'
Leonie said brightly, trying to sound more optimistic
than she felt and resisting the temptation to look at her
watch. If she didn't come up with the answer to Mrs
Kaminsky's problem soon, she was going to be late for
her lunch date.

'You told me that you were looking for a rug to go in
your main living-room. Can you tell me about the
room's colour-scheme—walls and curtains, etc?'

'Well, it's just been redecorated in shades of gold and
white by a simply *divine* young man I found. My
husband complained that it cost the earth, but I think it
looks great—really classy, if you know what I mean?'

As Mrs Kaminsky waved her hands enthusiastically in

the air, Leonie's eyes were drawn to a large turquoise and diamond ring on the older woman's finger.

'Of course!' Leonie clicked her teeth, annoyed with herself for not having thought of the answer to the problem before now. Smiling at the assistant, who had been waiting patiently for the last ten minutes, she pointed down to the end of the large, cavernous warehouse.

'Sorry to take so long, George. Can we look through that pile of large Qum rugs?' she said, before turning to her client. 'I know you've been thinking in terms of deep blues and dark reds, but I'm going to suggest that maybe you might decide to choose something more in harmony with your colour-scheme.'

Leading the way past the piles of rugs and carpets heaped one on top of the other, Leonie thought, as she had so often, that it was like walking through a treasure vault of precious gems; the incandescent glow of the jewelled silks almost dazzling beneath the strong arc lights set high in the ceiling.

'It was your ring which gave me the idea,' she explained to Mrs Kaminsky as the assistant began to turn over a fresh pile of carpets. 'These come from the holy city of Qum, in Iran. The political climate in that country is not too good at the moment, and so these pieces are becoming increasingly rare.'

Leonie bent down to stroke the soft, turquoise-coloured silk which formed a background to a garden of paradise design in gleaming tones of white, cream and gold.

'Now, *that's* more like it, honey!' the American woman enthused. 'I just love that shade of blue.'

'It's unique to all the pieces made in Qum. You'll never find that colour in any other Persian rug . . .'

'*A telephone call for Miss Elliot,*' a disembodied voice from a loudspeaker high on the wall cut into Leonie's words. '*Will Miss Leonie Elliot please come to reception.*'

'I can't think who...?' Leonie stood up, looking startled. 'I'm sorry, I'd better go and take the call. Don't hurry. Take plenty of time and look at all the various designs,' she instructed the older woman. 'I won't be long.'

Hurriedly threading her way across the floor and down the stairs towards the warehouse office, Leonie had a sudden moment of panic as she realised that it might be her mother on the phone, calling about Jade. Although the little girl was only four, her irrepressible high spirits had already resulted in a broken arm from falling out of a tree, and a severe burn on her leg due to experimenting with a forbidden box of matches.

Smiling briefly at the receptionist, she picked up the phone, sighing with relief to hear the voice of her secretary.

'Leonie?'

'Yes, Gwen, what's the problem?'

'Nothing dramatic,' Gwen said. 'But we've had an urgent request for a valuation. The client has to go abroad in two days' time, and is frantic at having to leave a valuable Heriz carpet uninsured. Can you manage to see the carpet at six o'clock tonight?'

Leonie grimaced. 'I was hoping to get home early for once. Any chance of my doing the valuation tomorrow morning?'

'I'm afraid not. It's the only time that the client has free, and both Henry and Philip are fully booked this afternoon. I'm still trying to sort out Mr Dimitri's diary. Goodness knows where I'm going to fit everyone in.'

'Yes, I know it's a problem,' Leonie agreed. The bad car accident which had kept her employer, Dimitri Kashan, away from the office for the last four weeks had meant an increased work-load for the other members of the firm. 'Okay, Gwen, I'll see to it—just as long as it is only an insurance valuation, and not someone wishing to arrange a sale. I simply wouldn't have enough time for that.'

'I've already made that point clear to the client,' her secretary assured her before rattling off an address in Mayfair. 'Just ring the doorbell and ask for Sheikh Samir, okay?'

'An Arab? You never said . . .' Leonie's voice trailed away as she realised that Gwen had put down the phone.

Thanking the receptionist and walking slowly out of the office, Leonie tried to banish a strange feeling of apprehension. How could there be any problem? Especially since she already had many clients from the oil-rich Arab states, who considered the purchase of oriental rugs and carpets to be a better investment than stocks and shares. Although, of course, the fact that she could speak Arabic was another reason why many of them preferred to deal with her firm.

Totally absorbed in her thoughts, it wasn't until Leonie felt a hand grasping her arm, that she realised she wasn't alone in the dusty corridor.

'Ah ha—at last! I've been hunting high and low for you, ever since my secretary said you were in the building.'

Leonie looked up, startled to see Jeff Powell's handsome face beaming down at her. 'I'm sorry . . .' She shook her head in confusion.

'What for? I only wish I could persuade you to leave Kashan's and join the wholesale trade,' he grinned. 'Maybe if you worked here, at Powell's, I wouldn't have such difficulty trying to convince you of my manifold charms! How about having dinner with me tonight?'

'I'm afraid I can't, I'm going to be tied up with business,' she murmured, moving aside as he tried to slip an arm about her waist.

'What a pity.' Jeff's mouth tightened slightly as he gazed at the girl standing beside him. Not only was she damn good at her job, but with her unusual colouring of large blue eyes set over a pale alabaster, almost translucent skin, surrounded by the fiery brilliance of her hair, she was a startlingly beautiful woman. A regular visitor to his warehouse during the last few years, she had steadfastly refused to respond to his advances. This had at first aroused disbelief and then, when he realised that she was impervious to his charm, he had become intrigued.

Without being vain, he was well aware of the fact that women found his blond good looks attractive, and being comparatively rich and successful, he had never had any trouble in finding girl-friends. He knew, from gossip within the trade, that there was a broken marriage in Leonie's background, and that she had a young daughter to support. However, she was only twenty-four, and he was certain that she must have had many relationships with other men; she was far too sexually attractive not to have done so. Why, then, did she insist on keeping him at a distance?

'What are you looking for, today?' he asked.

Leonie smiled. 'My client and I must have viewed practically every carpet in London! However, I think she's going to settle for a Qum rug—always provided your price isn't too steep.'

'You know that I'll always be happy to quote you a special price,' he said softly, moving closer to her slim frame.

'Yes, well . . . Oh my goodness—just look at the time!' Leonie murmured, hurriedly glancing down at her watch as she edged adroitly away. 'I must fly! Poor Mrs Kaminsky will wonder where I've got to,' she added over her shoulder as she hurried off down the corridor.

Jeff Powell stood looking after her disappearing figure for some moments, before giving a helpless shrug and returning to his office. Over an hour later he was still finding it difficult to concentrate on the business in hand, the vision of Leonie's lovely face coming between him and his work.

For her part, Leonie had no such problems. She was well used to dealing with the amorously-inclined Jeff Powells of this world, who more often than not regarded her as a challenge to their masculinity. She had, therefore, completely dismissed the handsome warehouse owner from her mind by the time she rejoined Mrs Kaminsky, who was happily enthusing over her choice of carpet.

It took some time to sort out the paperwork concerning the export of the carpet and Leonie was, as she had feared, already half an hour late for her lunch appointment when the taxi in which she was travelling turned into Jermyn Street. Entering the restaurant, she made her way over to the table where her old school friend, Sally, was waiting.

'I'm sorry to be so late, but it's just been one of those days,' Leonie said, sinking thankfully down on to a comfortable, velvet-covered chair. 'First of all the car wouldn't start this morning, then it was a matter of trundling from one warehouse to another, and just when I was about to leave the office, I had to take a long phone call from New York which... *Good gracious*! Do I spy a bottle of champagne?'

Sally laughed at the startled expression in her friend's wide blue eyes as a waiter placed the silver ice-bucket stand, containing a bottle of Dom Perignon, beside their table.

'*If* I can get a word in edgeways, I'd remind you that today is my birthday.'

'Oh, no! I completely forgot,' Leonie groaned.

'And I'm also celebrating a promotion at work. I'll have you know that you are in the privileged position of having lunch with Armstrong, Lord and Marshall's newest account executive!'

'Oh, Sally—how marvellous! I'm so pleased for you,' Leonie said, leaning back in her seat and beaming with delight. She knew that her friend had been hoping for this promotion within one of London's top advertising agencies, and it was good to know that all her hard work and talent had been recognised at last. 'Will you get a large rise in salary to maintain you in your new, exalted position?' she teased.

'I sincerely hope so—if only to pay for this lunch!' Sally retorted with a grin as the waiter opened the bottle and poured the champagne.

'Well, Happy Birthday, and congratulations,' Leonie said, raising her glass in a toast. 'Mmm, it's delicious— a real corpse reviver!' she added, savouring the cool dry taste of the sparkling liquid.

'You certainly don't look like a corpse,' Sally said, gazing with envy at the beautiful girl sitting beside her. 'What's the problem? Nothing wrong with Jade, I hope?'

'No, thank goodness. After her last escapade, she's been as good as gold. She now knows that climbing trees can lead to a fall—and a broken arm!' Leonie smiled as she remembered the indignant expression on her small daughter's face, when she realised she would have to wear a heavy plaster cast for some weeks. 'In fact, Jade's been angelic lately. Mainly, I suspect, because she's determined to be a bridesmaid at my mother's wedding!'

'It's only two weeks until the big day, isn't it? How are all the preparations going?'

'Fairly smoothly—so far! But Mother began panicking a month ago, about having to leave Jade and me alone in England, and I can't seem to persuade her to stop worrying.'

An American, Leonie's father had been a senior executive with an oil company based in Tehran. The Shah's departure and the rise of the Ayatollahs had left Iran in a ferment, and John Elliot had opted to take early retirement, deciding to live in England where Leonie, aged fourteen, was still at boarding school. The fact that his wife was English and had many relatives in the country was also a deciding factor in his decision, and it was tragic that he should have died so shortly after moving into their new home in London.

Over the past ten years, Leonie's mother had settled down to a reasonably contented widowhood when, quite suddenly out of the blue, a friend of her father's over on a visit from the United States had decided to round off his holiday by calling to see Mrs Elliot. That had been three months ago, and with what seemed the speed of light, Clifford T. Brownlow and her mother had decided to get married. Leonie thoroughly approved of her prospective stepfather, and of his desire to take her mother back to his home in Florida after the wedding. The only problem had been Mrs Elliot's increasing concern about Leonie and Jade's future.

'It wouldn't be so bad if you had a nice, reliable nanny,' her mother had said a few weeks ago. 'I know you've contacted all the agencies, darling, but if you can't find someone, what are you going to do?'

'I'll manage somehow,' Leonie murmured soothingly. 'There's no need to worry.'

'Well, I can't help worrying. I've been pleased to do what I can, looking after Jade while you've been at work—but even you must realise that it hasn't been an ideal situation. Whether you'll admit it or not,' Mrs Elliot added firmly, 'the plain truth is that Jade is a bright, intelligent little girl who needs a father.'

'Oh, Mother!' Leonie groaned. 'Don't let's go through it all again! My marriage was over almost before it began, for heaven's sake. I know your views on the sanctity of marriage, but all I want is a divorce!'

Mrs Elliot sighed heavily. 'I don't approve of your getting a divorce, of course, but I thought that Badyr had agreed . . .'

'The letter to my solicitor from Dhoman was quite specific. It said that he "might be prepared to consider such a course of action"—but only if I'd agree to meet him and discuss the matter.' Leonie shrugged. 'There's no way I can possibly agree to that. Badyr doesn't know about Jade, and I daren't take the risk of his finding out about her.'

'I've always said that it was quite wrong of you not to tell Badyr about his child,' her mother said stubbornly. 'He has a legal right to know about his daughter, and your fears that he would take her away from you are quite ridiculous.'

Leonie had suppressed a sharp retort. There was little point in resurrecting all the old arguments as to why she had not informed Badyr about Jade. He had been under arrest in Dhoman when his daughter was born, and couldn't have received the message in any case. By the time his despotic old father had been despatched into exile, she had heard and read about too many cases of Arab fathers snatching their children and disappearing without trace, to be able to feel that she could take the risk.

At the thought of Jade's possible abduction, Leonie could feel her stomach contract with panic. There was absolutely no doubt in her mind that she had made the right decision—however morally wrong it might be— not to have told her husband about their daughter. All she had to do was to wait for another year, and then she could get a divorce with or without Badyr's consent. Not that she had any intention of marrying again—far from it! That one, brief experience, had been quite enough to put her off matrimony for life.

'Hey! What are you trying to do—jab that steak to death?'

'What . . .?' Leonie looked up, startled out of her bitter, introspective thoughts by Sally's laughing comment. 'I was just . . . er . . . well, I was just thinking that I must make a greater effort to find a nanny to look after Jade while I'm at work. God knows what will happen to the business if I don't.'

'When I last saw you, your employer had just been carted off to hospital. Has it caused a lot of extra work?'

'And how!' Leonie gave a mock groan. 'Business is

booming at the moment—which is obviously good for the firm, and since Dimitri has placed me in overall charge during his absence, I've found myself run off my feet. However, if I'm to be honest,' she added with a grin, 'I have to admit that I'm loving every chaotic moment!'

Sally laughed and then looked thoughtfully down at the table as she fiddled with the stem of her glass. 'I can see that you are frightfully busy, but I would be grateful if—well, if you could find the time to do me a favour.'

'Yes, of course I will, if I can.'

'Well, it isn't for me, exactly . . .' Her friend paused and then took the plunge. 'I realise I may be treading on painful memories, but the fact is that one of the girls sharing my apartment has gone and got herself engaged to a Prince from Saudi Arabia.'

'Oh Lord!'

'Yes, my sentiments exactly! However, I wondered if you could have a talk to her. The other two girls and I have tried to warn her about the pitfalls, but she simply won't listen. She may be in love with the man, of course, but we suspect that it's much more likely that she's simply dazzled out of her mind by his fast sports car, dining at the Ritz practically every night, and the expensive, fabulous jewellery he's been throwing in her direction.'

Leonie sighed heavily. 'It's so difficult, isn't it? How on earth do you explain to someone—especially if they think that they're madly in love—the differences between East and West; the drastic culture-shock she's likely to experience? I know that I refused to listen to any advice at the time, however well intentioned.'

'I read somewhere that Saudi Arabia has by far the strictest regime, as far as women are concerned. Is that right?' Sally asked.

'Yes. Most of the Gulf states are fairly liberal, but all women living in Saudi Arabia—of whatever nationality—must conform to very strict rules. For instance:

she won't be able to work, or drive a car.' Leonie ticked
the items off on her fingers. 'Neither can she leave her
house, even for a simple thing like going to the shops—
not unless she is accompanied by a male relative. In
effect, it means that your friend will be a prisoner in her
home for very long periods of time. What's more, she'll
probably see very little of her husband. He's more than
likely to dump his new wife with his mother, and then
spend most of his time with his male friends. So, unless
she can speak Arabic, she will find herself living a silent,
lonely life among complete strangers.'

'Oh, my!' Sally shuddered. 'It sounds horrific!'

'Well, yes, it is—if you've been brought up to a life of
freedom in the Western hemisphere. However, I
suppose that if you and I had been born in Arabia, and
raised strictly according to the Moslem faith, we would
think it was a perfectly normal and generally happy
way of life.'

'Did you find ... I mean, was your existence in
Dhoman as bad as that?' Sally looked at her with
concern.

'Good gracious no!' Leonie smiled bitterly. 'Living in
Saudi Arabia would have been a picnic compared to the
medieval harem in which I found myself!'

'But I thought ... surely, now that your husband is a
king, or whatever ...'

'Sultan,' Leonie corrected her. 'His Majesty, Sultan
Badyr ibn Raschid Al Hamad, to be precise! He ousted
his old father from the throne some years ago—and I
hope he's enjoying himself,' she added grimly. 'Because,
believe me, a more backward, hopelessly archaic
country would be hard to find! God knows, I was only
there for a short time, but as far as I'm concerned it was
the worst three months of my entire life!'

Although they had been friends for years, Sally had
been abroad when Leonie had got married and knew
very little about her husband, or the life she had led in
the South Arabian Kingdom of Dhoman. She was only

aware that the experience had left her friend withdrawn and silent on the subject: Leonie having always made it very clear that she didn't want to talk about her brief marriage.

'I had no idea . . .! I mean, I wouldn't have brought up the subject if I'd known . . .' Sally muttered, wishing that she had kept her mouth shut.

'There's no need to worry, and I'll certainly do what I can to persuade your friend to take a long hard look at the life in front of her! As far as my marriage is concerned,' Leonie said crisply, 'it ended nearly five years ago and now, when I look back, I can appreciate some of the good things about the country and the people—even if I couldn't see it at the time.'

She paused as she tried to find words to express the complex ideology of the East. 'It's so totally alien to everything we in the West have been brought up to believe in—it's a completely different way of life. For instance, an Arab husband would be astounded and deeply offended if you accused him of being cruel to his wife by keeping her incarcerated inside her home. The men are taught to cherish and protect their women, and what you and I would definitely think of as a jail sentence, they regard as warm, loving care.' She shrugged. 'I suppose it's only fair to say that they do have a tremendous feeling of close family unity, a solidarity and fierce pride, not only in their immediate family, but also in their country.'

'I still think that the life sounds simply awful! What we need is another glass of champagne,' Sally said firmly, catching the eye of a passing waiter. 'And while I'm on the subject, I've got some friends coming in for a drink early this evening, why don't you call by on your way back from work?'

Leonie shook her head regretfully. 'I'd love to, but I have an appointment to value a carpet at six o'clock. Besides, I always try to be home reasonably early, so that I can bath Jade—it's the one part of the day when we can spend some time together.'

'There's no doubt about the fact that motherhood suits you,' Sally assured her with a grin. 'If I could have a guarantee that I'd look as good as you do, I might be tempted to get married and have a baby!'

'Is Robert Armstrong still trying to persuade you to name the day?' Leonie queried, referring to her friend's long-standing relationship with her boss.

'Well . . .' Sally blushed. 'I'm getting to the point when I think I might give him the shock of his life, and agree to marry him!'

'Goodness! What's brought on this change of heart?'

'Reaching twenty-five!' Sally moaned, staring gloomily down at the bubbles in her glass.

'You poor old, middle-aged hag!' Leonie laughed as she rose to leave. 'I'll see you and your parents at Mum's wedding of course, but in the meantime, I should snap up Robert while the going's good. You know that you are both crazy about each other—so say "yes" and be happy, hmm?' She bent down to kiss her friend's cheek. 'I'd like to stay longer and help you to drown your sorrows, but I've got a million things to do back at the office.'

She hadn't been exaggerating, Leonie told herself some hours later as she paid off a taxi and looked at the impressive exterior of the large town house. The telephone had never stopped ringing all afternoon, and it had been a scramble to get here on time for her six o'clock appointment.

'I believe Sheikh Samir is expecting me,' she said as the door was opened by a portly butler, dressed in a black coat and striped trousers. With a deep bow he silently conducted her across the black and white marble hall and up a wide staircase to the first floor of the large building. Knocking discreetly on a large pair of doors, he pushed them open and then stood aside to allow her to enter the room.

My goodness—it's the size of a ballroom! Leonie thought, hardly given time to take in the proportions of the enormous room as a short, dark-haired young man came forward to greet her.

'Sheikh Samir?'

'I am delighted to make your acquaintance, Miss—er—Elliot,' he murmured, bowing his head over her hand and then gesturing towards the large carpet lying beneath a brilliantly lit chandelier.

Leonie knew of no precise formula for analysing the 'quality' of a rug, but by any criteria the deep, glowing pool at her feet had to be one of the finest antique carpets she had ever seen. Totally immersed, she bent down to examine it closer, delighting in the exquisite workmanship and in the subtle tones of the jewelled silk colours, all in perfect harmony. A breathtakingly beautiful carpet, with its pile length, fringes and borders all as good as new—it was a masterpiece!

'This is obviously an extremely valuable rug,' she said as she rose to her feet, unable to tear her eyes away from such perfection. 'Forgive me for being blunt, Sheikh Samir, but I must point out that you have been taking a considerable risk in not insuring such a piece before now, and I must urge you to contact an insurance broker first thing tomorrow morning. I will, of course, measure it in a moment and give you a firm valuation, but I can tell you straight away that a rug in this condition would fetch at least a thousand pounds a square foot.'

Leonie forced herself to turn away from the carpet, anxious to impress upon the Sheikh just what a precious object he owned. But to her bewilderment, he seemed to have vanished into thin air. Puzzled, she looked about her, before a movement in a dark corner of the room attracted her attention.

Still amazed at the discovery of such a superb example of the rug-makers' art, Leonie frowned, peering into the grey shadows which lay beyond the brilliant pool of light over the carpet. A sudden shiver of fright ran down her spine, her eyes widening with shock at the sight of the tall figure walking slowly towards her.

'B-Badyr . . .?'

Her incredulous, hoarse whisper reverberated about the enormous room, echoing in her ears as she closed her dazed eyes for a moment. It couldn't be! It simply wasn't possible! What on earth was her husband doing here? And in London, of all places?

CHAPTER TWO

'WELL, well. What a pleasure it is to see you again, my dear Leonie. It has been a long time, has it not?'

Oh, dear God! There was no mistaking that deep, faintly accented and coolly ironic tone of voice. Leonie put out a hand to grab the top of a nearby chair for support, her whole body shaking with tension as if in the grip of a raging fever. Fighting to control her ragged breathing, she gazed with stupefaction at the man she hadn't seen for almost five years.

It was . . . yes, of course it was Badyr. And yet, as her eyes swept over the man who had now come to a halt on the other side of the carpet, it seemed as if she were looking at a complete stranger.

Leonie stared blankly at his tall figure. Her dazed vision filled with the sight of broad shoulders tapering to slim hips elegantly attired in an expensively tailored dark suit, the impeccable fit emphasising the lean tautness of the body that she remembered so well. No, it wasn't his tall frame that was so unfamiliar. Forcing herself to raise her eyes from his immaculate white shirt, contrasting sharply against the brown column of his neck, she felt the colour drain from her face for a second time.

What on earth had happened to Badyr? There seemed to be nothing she could do to hide her shock and confusion as she gazed at the black patch covering his left eye, from which a deep scar carved its way down over his tanned cheek to the line of his jaw. The raven's-wing blackness of his hair, lying thick and smooth against his well-shaped head before curling over the collar of his suit, was the only instantly recognisable feature that she could recall. It was almost impossible to reconcile the memory of her husband's lazy charm, his handsome appearance and warm personality, with the harsh, rugged features and physically dangerous aura projected so strongly by this ... this man, whose one, glittering dark eye was subjecting her to a slow, silent appraisal that almost scorched her skin.

'W-what are you d-doing here ...?' she stuttered, trying to pull her distraught mind together.

'Such a warm welcome after all these years!' Badyr murmured sardonically. 'Perhaps I felt it was about time that we should meet to discuss various matters, hmm?'

'There's nothing ... nothing for us to discuss—other than a divorce, of course,' she retorted, clasping her hands together to hide their trembling agitation.

'I can think of one or two other items,' he drawled. 'However, if you particularly wish to talk about the termination of our marriage, then I am prepared to hear what you have to say.'

Leonie gasped, anger and resentment sweeping through her body at his casual condescension, the patronising note in his voice. How dare he treat her like this? It wasn't her fault that she had been forced to flee from Dhoman all those years ago. Never once, in all that time, had he even bothered to contact her. And now, suddenly appearing from nowhere like a genie from a bottle ... Her stomach lurched, apprehension and a dawning realisation of the truth welling up like sickness inside her.

'Sheikh Samir ...?' she whispered.

'My aide-de-camp.'

'And ... and the carpet?'

Badyr gave a negligent shrug, moving with lithe grace to lean against the edge of a table. 'It was merely a convenient bait to draw you within my orbit—nothing more.'

Leonie shook her head in confusion, waving away his words with a gesure of irritation. 'That carpet is priceless, for heaven's sake! I simply don't understand what's going on. It . . . it doesn't make sense!'

'On the contrary, it makes excellent sense.' The sensual curve of his mouth twisted in a wry smile. 'For over a year, your solicitor has been repeatedly told that I wished to talk to you personally, face to face, and each time I was informed that you would not agree to such a meeting. I therefore decided to take matters into my own hands—and here you are! What a fortunate man I am,' he added with cynical amusement, 'to have the opportunity of at last being able to see my—er—darling wife.'

I'm not your darling wife! she wanted to scream, feeling that she had somehow strayed into a nightmare. With a nervous, unconscious movement, she raised her hand to smooth away a stray tendril, which had fallen down from the heavy knot of hair on top of her head. Her heart thudded in her chest as she felt his gaze linger on the curve of her breasts, thrown into prominence by her action. Leonie's cheeks grew hot and flushed beneath his analytical scrutiny.

When he spoke again, the tone of his voice was subtly different. It contained a new, personal warmth which sent shivers feathering down her spine. 'You are thinner than I remembered, Leonie. It doesn't suit you.'

'We're not here to discuss my figure,' she snapped nervously. 'And . . . and why are we meeting in this building, anyway?'

'It would, of course, have been more convenient for us to have met in my suite at Claridges. However, since I wished to minimise the chances of your discovering my intentions,' he added with a mocking grin, 'I think that this place has served its purpose admirably.'

Had he flown over from Dhoman especially to see her? It seemed as though he was going to let her have a divorce, but if so, why had he gone to such trouble, when all he had to do was to send a letter of agreement to her solicitor? Stiff with tension, she glanced warily at him through her eyelashes as he stood up and looked slowly around the enormous room.

'A charming building, is it not?' he murmured blandly. 'I have appointed one of my sheikhs to be the new Dhomani Ambassador, and he presents his credentials to the Court of St James next week. I think he will be very comfortable here, don't you?'

Leonie gritted her teeth, shaking with suppressed anger and frustration at the underlying note of laughter in his voice. It was clear that Badyr was amusing himself at her expense, undoubtedly taking his revenge for her adamant refusal to meet him. As the ruling Sultan of Dhoman, and probably every bit as autocratic a dictator as his old father before him, the comfort of his Ambassador was likely to be a long way down his list of priorities!

Suddenly, Leonie decided that she had had enough of this confrontation. If he wanted to discuss their divorce, he could do it with her lawyer. The shock of seeing him again, especially the dramatic change in his appearance effected by the black eye-patch and the deep scar running down his cheek, had initially unnerved her. However, she was beginning to recover her equilibrium. There was no reason on earth why she should have to stand here while Badyr played whatever cat-and-mouse game he had in mind.

'I don't wish to see you again, and I suggest that any further communications between us are dealt with by our respective solicitors,' she said as firmly as she could, turning to walk over to the door.

'Not so fast, my dear Leonie!' He moved swiftly to catch hold of her arm. 'Just where do you think you are going, hmm?'

She glared up at the harsh, indomitable expression on Badyr's face, conscious of her erratic heartbeat at his close proximity.

'Take your hands off me!' she snapped, trying to break free of his grip.

'There was a time when you hungered for my touch,' he murmured softly. 'Or have you forgotten?'

'I . . . I've forgotten everything,' she retorted quickly, inwardly cursing the husky, breathless note in her voice.

'Really?' His lips curved into a sardonic smile. 'Let us see, hmm?'

'*No . . .!*' She found herself jerked swiftly into his arms, her exclamation of horrified denial stifled as his mouth possessed hers in a hard, determined fashion. Struggling against the arms which tightened about her like bands of steel, frantically trying to push him away, she was aware of a treacherous warmth invading her limbs beneath the kiss that burned and demanded her submission.

Gradually and imperceptibly the cruel, ruthless pressure eased, his lips becoming warm and persuasive as they softly coaxed and teased away all resistance. Her pulse seemed to be racing out of control, her slim figure shaking with long-suppressed emotions and lost beneath a sudden tidal wave of desire; totally unable to prevent herself from passionately responding to the sensual, erotic mastery of his tongue as he savoured the inner sweetness of her mouth. With a low, husky moan, Leonie's arms tightened about his neck, her fingers burying themselves convulsively in his thick black hair. The evocative, musky scent of his cologne filled her nostrils, a raging excitement seizing her body at the fierce possession of Badyr's embrace and the evidence, in the hard muscled thighs pressed so closely to hers, of his own arousal.

Drowning in a pool of dark passion, she shivered as his mouth trailed slowly down the long column of her neck, to seek the scented hollows at the base of her throat. It was some moments before her eyelids fluttered open, the light from the chandelier almost dazzling her. Through that blinding brilliance she saw Badyr looking down at her, his mouth twisted in a slight, ironic smile.

'It would appear that you have not entirely forgotten *everything*, my dear Leonie, hmm?'

Leonie felt sick with self-disgust, a flush of deep crimson covering her face as she realised just how easily she had succumbed to Badyr's embrace. He had always been able to arouse her, even when she had been a miserably unhappy prisoner of the harem in Dhoman. The physical attraction between them had been the strongest, most potent part of their relationship; a bond, it would seem, as yet unbroken by the separate lives they had led during the last five years.

She fought against acknowledging the fact. Furious with herself, and him, she quickly broke away from the loose grip of his encircling arms.

'If you think that ... that kiss solved anything, or meant a thing to me, you are sadly mistaken!' she ground out savagely.

Turning away from Badyr's piercing gaze, she attempted to control her nervously shaking hands as she tucked her white silk blouse back inside the waistband of her navy blue skirt. God knows what her hair looked like, she thought helplessly, and she didn't suppose she had a shred of make-up left on her face. But this was hardly the time or the place to worry about such unimportant details. She must ... she simply must leave this house as quickly as she possibly could.

Ignoring her words, Badyr walked over to pull an embroidered bell-rope hanging down the side of a wall. 'I suggest that we now leave. I have ordered dinner to be served in my suite at the hotel, where we can continue our—er—discussion in more comfortable surroundings.'

'There is nothing to discuss—nothing that our two lawyers can't sort out between them. I'm leaving now,' she added firmly. 'And there is no reason why we should have to meet ever again.'

'I'm afraid, my dear Leonie, that it isn't that simple. I have some personal matters that I wish to discuss with you, and if you adamantly refuse to join me for dinner, then I will simply have to accompany you to your home.'

'No ...!'

'Why not? I would be interested to see your house.' He smiled lazily at the girl who was staring at him in consternation. 'You are living with your mother, I understand.'

'It ... er ... it wouldn't be ... er ... at all convenient for you to call at my home,' she muttered quickly. She could feel beads of perspiration breaking out on her forehead at the thought of his finding out about Jade.

'What a pity. I have many fond memories of your charming mother, and would have enjoyed meeting her again.'

'No ... well, I'm afraid that she ... she's in bad health at the moment,' Leonie improvised swiftly. 'She's ... er ... she's had the flu, and ... um ... still hasn't recovered.'

'Really? Then I must surely pray for her swift recovery.'

Leonie's head jerked up at the deep, sardonic note of amusement in his voice. It might be her imagination, but for a moment it had seemed as if his shoulders had been shaking with inner laughter. *The damn man!* He might not realise it, but he had somehow managed to completely outmanoeuvre her. If she didn't go and have dinner with him, he was quite capable of turning up at her home, despite any excuse she might be able to think of.

As she hesitated, desperately trying to think of a way out of her dilemma, there was a knock on the door and Sheikh Samir entered the room.

'The chauffeur awaits your pleasure, Majesty,' he murmured, being careful not to look in her direction as he bowed deeply to Badyr.

'Well, Leonie,' Badyr purred dangerously. 'Which is

it to be? Dinner at my hotel, or do I instruct the
chauffeur to take us both back to your house, hmm?'

Locking the door of the palatial bathroom firmly
behind her, Leonie gave a heavy sigh as she slipped off
the jacket of her navy blue suit, and went over to sit
down on a stool in front of the marble-topped dressing-
table.

There never had been any choice, had there? Not
really. There had been no alternative to having dinner
here in the hotel with Badyr, since she couldn't possibly
risk his finding out about Jade. She had taken such
pains over the last five years, first to hide her pregnancy
and then her daughter, that she couldn't possibly allow
him to discover the truth.

Resting her chin in the palms of her hands, she stared
gloomily into the mirror. What a mess! And she looked
a mess too, she told herself, glumly taking out the
tortoiseshell combs which held her hair in place on top
of her head. Shaking the thick mass of curly red-gold
hair free, she opened her purse, relieved to see that it
held her brush and comb as well as her make-up bag.

Leonie's lips twisted in a wry, ironic smile as she
looked around at the pale beige marble walls, the gold
taps and what seemed an enormous collection of
brilliantly lit mirrors reflecting every inch of the huge,
luxurious bathroom. What it was to be the reigning
Sultan of an oil-rich, desert state! Not that she wanted
any part of it. She had experienced life locked inside a
gilded cage, and she knew only too well that wealth,
position and privilege meant nothing without freedom.
During her incarceration in Dhoman, she had learnt
for the first time just what a precious commodity
freedom was—something she hadn't realised until it had
been taken away.

Leonie took a deep dreath and attempted to pull
herself together. There was no point in being so gloomy
and introspective about her past life. That was now well

behind her, thank goodness, and after she and Badyr
had raked over the cold ashes of their marriage tonight,
she would be free of Dhoman and all it stood for.

Drawing a brush through the heavy thickness of her
curly hair, she noticed for the first time the delicately
engraved, jewelled flask placed beneath the dressing-
table mirror. Putting out a hand to admire the
craftsmanship of the object designed in the shape of a
khanjar, the curved ceremonial dagger worn by
Dhomani men, her eyes widened as she realised it was
made from solid gold. Removing the stopper and
inhaling the rich aroma of frankincense, sandalwood,
musk and other spices, Leonie instantly recognised the
scent of *Amouage*, the mind-bogglingly expensive
cologne used by Badyr.

Suddenly, all the conflicting emotions she had felt in
his arms earlier that evening rose up to torment her.
There seemed little she could do to banish the
throbbing, sick excitement in the pit of her stomach as
she remembered the way he had crushed her so tightly
against his hard chest. The sensual touch of his lips and
. . . With a soft moan, Leonie leapt to her feet and
rushed over to splash her face with cold water, roughly
towelling it dry as she tried to expunge the visions from
her mind.

It had just been an unfortunate accident, that was all,
she assured herself hurriedly. It would never, ever,
happen again—of course it wouldn't! Badyr had only
been proving to his own satisfaction, if not hers, that he
was still an attractive man. A fact which, despite that
patch and scar on his face, she was quite prepared to
admit. But so what? Her fingers trembled as she swept
up her hair and jabbed the combs into her scalp. She
couldn't care less whom he kissed or made love to—just
as long as it wasn't her—right? The word 'wrong'
seemed to be hovering at the back of her mind, but she
ruthlessly crushed such a nonsensical thought and
quickly finished making up her face.

Giving herself a swift appraisal in the mirror, she was satisfied that the severe cut of her navy blue suit, and the v-necked white silk blouse, looked businesslike and efficient. The perfect outfit in which to discuss a divorce, she told herself, briskly walking over to unlock the door.

Unfortunately, it didn't seem as if Badyr took quite the same view. 'You look ravishing, as always!' he murmured, handing her a glass of champagne as she entered the large sitting-room.

'Aren't you going to have a drink?' she asked nervously, ignoring his compliment and warily noting the warm, intimate atmosphere conveyed by the deep piled carpet and the discreet lighting.

'In my present position, I feel that I must set a good example and follow the precepts laid down by my religion,' he said with a wry smile.

'If you are such a good Moslem,' Leonie said, swiftly tossing the Dutch courage down her throat, 'why don't you just say, "I divorce you" three times, and fly home to Dhoman? Our lawyers can deal with any paperwork, and then we'll both be happy.'

'No, I would not be happy, Leonie. That is not what I want,' he said.

'Okay,' she sighed. 'What *do* you want? What are you doing over here in London? And why, when our marriage is dead and buried, should I have been practically blackmailed into coming to this hotel?'

'Why do you not sit down and make yourself comfortable?' He waved towards one of the several deep-seated sofas that decorated the room.

'I prefer to stand,' she retorted mutinously.

Badyr shrugged, walking slowly over to seat himself in a wide leather armchair. 'You have asked me why I am here, in London,' he said softly, brushing an invisible speck of dust off his sleeve. 'It is really very simple, my dear Leonie. Don't you think that it is time that my daughter and I became acquainted with each other, hmm?'

Leonie gasped in horror, the breath driven from her lungs as if she had received a hard blow to the solar plexus. 'Your . . . your d-daughter?' she whispered, the blood draining from her face.

'Sit down,' he commanded sharply as she swayed with shock. 'Did you really think that you could keep it a secret from me?' he added quietly as her legs gave way and she sank down into a chair. 'I may have been under house arrest at the time, but I can assure you that I was well aware of what was happening in the rest of the country,' he said drily. 'I imagine that I knew of your pregnancy almost as soon as you did.'

'But . . . but why did you never get in touch with me? I never had a word from you, not from the moment you were arrested and taken away!' she protested.

'I couldn't risk it. You must remember how it was, Leonie. My father was firmly in the grip of senile dementia, and if he had found out about your pregnancy none of us would have been safe.'

'But surely . . .'

'I am speaking the truth, believe me,' Badyr assured her. 'He would have kept you under close supervision and then, if you had produced a son, my life wouldn't have been worth a damn! I had no idea what would happen to you, either. Which was why I had to arrange your immediate departure from Dhoman. At least there are proper hospitals in the West,' he added bitterly. 'As you know, the only medical care in the country at that time was the small surgery run by some Americans.'

'I—I had no idea that it was you who arranged my escape.' Leonie lay back in her chair, resting her head against the cushions. Her brain felt as if it had been battered into insensibility, totally stunned by the shocks she had sustained that day. 'But after the coup—after your father was deposed—why didn't you get in touch with me then?'

Badyr sighed. 'One of the main reasons for the coup was to take the reins of the country into my own hands.

Ignored by my father, the Marxist rebels had already
gained control of the western part of Dhoman, and
were being heavily supplied with men and weapons
from both Russia and China. My agents told me that
you had reverted to your maiden name, and I decided
that you and the child would be safest if there was no
contact between us. If certain "friends" of the rebels
had known of your existence, there was a very real
possibility of your both being kidnapped. I had no
intention of submitting to that sort of blackmail,' he
added grimly.

'The plain fact, my dear Leonie, is that for the last
four years I have been fully occupied. Every ounce of
my time and energy has been spent trying to drag my
country away from its medieval condition, and into the
twentieth century. Moreover, as Commander in Chief
of the forces under my command, I had a nasty, brutal
war to fight. I could not, therefore, afford to be
distracted by the soft charms of either my wife or my
daughter!'

He paused, the seconds slipping by as he regarded the
trembling figure of the beautiful girl seated across the
room. Her wide, sapphire-blue eyes stared blankly back
at him from a face which seemed to be drained of all colour.

Leonie shifted uneasily under the intensity of his
gaze, her head throbbing as she tried to grapple with
the fact that Badyr had always known about Jade. No
matter how hard she tried, Leonie couldn't seem to
think constructively. Her mind seemed to have become
numb, her brain an empty void.

Badyr rose and went over to lean against the marble
fireplace. 'Now that I have at last defeated the rebels—
thanks mainly to the British troops kindly lent to me by
the British Government—Dhoman is now at peace.' He
smiled wryly. 'Of course, there is still a lifetime of work
to be done in the country, building roads, hospitals and
schools for instance, but I can at last afford to sit back
and relax somewhat.'

'Is that how you came by the ... er ... scar? In the war, I mean,' she muttered.

He gave a wry laugh. 'Alas, nothing so heroic! Having decided that my father really must be deposed, for the sake of Dhoman if not for anything else, I and my supporters arranged for a bloodless coup to take place. It was, of course, up to me to tell my father that his days as a ruler were over—not one of the most pleasant duties I have had to perform!' He came over to pour her another glass of champagne.

'Unfortunately, my father did not greet the decision with—er—enthusiasm, and I was careless enough to allow him to draw his ceremonial sword on me. I hate to think what my old instructor at Sandhurst would have said about letting myself be surprised like that!' He smiled and ruefully shook his head. 'However, I could not possibly bring myself to shoot the man who had given me birth, and so I attempted to talk him out of taking any foolish action. Whereupon, he promptly aimed a blow at my head! Of course, my father was quickly disarmed by the men under my command; the only lasting result of the fracas was that I needed twenty stitches in my face—and I suffer from a case of permanent double vision from the blow to my temple.'

Leonie winced, expecting some dreadful revelation as he raised his hand and removed the black patch. To her surprise, both the eyes gleaming at her from beneath their heavy lids appeared to be perfectly normal.

'You see?' Badyr gave her a wry smile. 'I merely wear this patch to correct my double vision. I have seen many eye specialists, and they tell me that there is nothing they can do.' He paused. 'Do you find my appearance so very terrible, Leonie?'

'No, no, not at all,' she muttered. What on earth were they doing—sitting here and calmly discussing his eye-patch, for heaven's sake? He had always been physically very attractive, and now with that patch and scar he seemed doubly so. Leonie knew that most women of her acquaintance would find such a dangerous, pirate-like image almost irresistible! And undoubtedly there had been many women in the last five years, she told herself sourly, before striving to banish such errant thoughts from her mind. Far more to the point was her concern about Jade.

'We must now talk about my daughter,' Badyr said, echoing her own thoughts with uncanny clairvoyance.

There was a long silence which seemed to reverberate around the room, Leonie stared determinedly down at the glass tightly clasped in her hands, which were shaking as if she had the palsy.

'I don't see that there is very much to discuss,' she murmured at last. 'You will want to see her, of course, but ...' She faltered as Badyr gave a harsh bark of sardonic laughter.

'Oh, yes, Leonie. I fully intend to see Jade! Earlier in our conversation you asked me what it was that I wanted. Well, I must tell you that I want my daughter. I have come over here to London, with the express intention of taking her back to live with me in Dhoman.'

'You ... you can't take Jade away from me—*you can't!*' she whispered, almost fainting at the wave of blind panic which ran like quicksilver through her trembling body.

'I do not intend to, of course. But if the necessity arose ...? Yes, I can see no difficulty. The courts might well award me care and custody,' Badyr drawled smoothly. 'But if that action should fail, I would merely remove her from this country.'

'*No!*'

'No? Can you guarantee to guard her for every moment of every day? I think not!'

'You monster! I won't let you take her away from me!' she cried, jumping to her feet. 'Jade has never even

seen you, for heaven's sake. She would be terrified!'
Leonie gazed at him with horror, unable to say any
more for the hard lump obstructing her throat.

'Calm down, Leonie!' Badyr rose to his feet, walking
swiftly over to place his hands firmly on her shoulders.
'I have already said that I do not intend to take Jade
away from you.'

'Then why did you mention the courts and threaten
to abduct her?' she gasped, her whole body racked with
pain.

'I wanted you to understand that I am very serious
about the return of my daughter.'

'*Serious?* I am hardly likely to find your words
amusing, am I?' she cried, unable to prevent the helpless
tears from coursing down her cheeks.

'Come, there is no need to weep,' Badyr murmured
softly, taking her trembling body into his arms. 'Yes, I
want my daughter—but I also want you,' he added,
removing a handkerchief from his pocket and gently
wiping her eyes.

'Me? You want me to return to Dhoman?' She gave a
shrill, hysterical laugh as she abruptly broke away from
his embrace. '*You must be mad!*'

He shook his head. 'No, I am very sane. I wish to live
with my wife and daughter by my side. Is that so
strange?'

'Never, under any circumstances, could I possibly
face going to live in Dhoman again. Once was enough!'

'In that case, my dear Leonie, you must be prepared
to lose your child.'

The chilling finality of his words hit her like a blow.
'For God's sake, Badyr, you can't mean it? What have I
ever done to deserve such a terrible punishment? You
can't be so ... s-so c-cruel!' Tears of utter desolation
streamed down her cheeks as she clutched frantically at
his arm. 'Don't do this to me ... please don't take away
my little girl ...' she sobbed.

'Compose yourself, Leonie!' he demanded sternly, a

muscle beating in his clenched jaw. 'I am not intending to take Jade from you, that would indeed be cruel.'

'But you said . . .'

'I said I wished you both to return with me to Dhoman. If you refuse to come, then it is *you* who will be abandoning our child.'

'I can't bear the thought of going back there!' she wailed helplessly as Badyr led her shaking figure over to a sofa. 'You know how awful it was for me—who better? I—I've never been so desperately unhappy in my whole life. Shut away in that dreadful, medieval fortress . . .' Leonie buried her face in her hands, her slim figure shuddering at the bitter memories she had tried so hard to forget.

'That was all in the past. You would find your position in Dhoman quite different now,' he replied evenly, seating himself on the sofa beside her. 'As my wife, you will have your own palace and your own servants. You will be free to come and go as you wish, although for your own safety I would insist on your having a bodyguard with you at all times. There are still one or two rebels at large,' he explained. 'The guards would only be there for your own protection.'

'It still sounds like the same old Dhoman that I loved to hate!' she retorted, fiercely blowing her nose. 'And why now? Why this sudden desire for your child, when you've managed to ignore us all these years?'

Badyr gave an impatient sigh. 'I have spent a good part of the evening so far, explaining exactly why I "ignored" you and my daughter.'

'Hogwash!' she lashed back angrily. 'I can read the papers, you know! That war of yours was finished a good year ago, so why the sudden interest in reclaiming your daughter, huh?'

'I am touched to learn that you have been taking such an interest in the affairs of my country,' he drawled with heavy sarcasm. 'However, your mother's wedding has merely brought forward my plans. I always intended that both you and Jade should return to Dhoman.'

'My—my mother's wedding?' Leonie looked at him in astonishment.

He shrugged. 'Of course. When your mother contacted me ...'

'She *what* ...!'

'Your mother was very worried about the future of yourself and the child. It was quite right and proper that she should let me know how matters stood, and she was absolutely correct in assuming that I would take responsibility for you both.'

'Oh God! How could she do this to me?' Leonie wailed, jumping to her feet in trembling agitation. 'No wonder you were laughing your head off back at the Embassy—you knew very well that my mother wasn't ill—you swine!'

Badyr's lips curved into a sardonic smile. 'Yes, I must confess to having been amused by your—er—inventiveness!'

'I bet you were! Well, let me tell you that Jade and I need you like a hole in the head—far less, in fact! Jade will be going to school in about six months' time and ... I've got a job that I love. You can't ...'

'I am well aware of your success in the wholesale oriental rug market,' he murmured blandly. 'I have been pleased to hear of how well you have progressed with your firm, and of Dimitri Kashan's trust and confidence in your ability.'

Leonie glared at him, her hackles rising at his condescending tone of voice. 'Don't you patronise me— you ... you bloody man! Yes, I'm good at my job, and if I'm successful it's due solely to my own effort and hard work. I don't need you, or your millions, and I've absolutely no intention of throwing up my career and going back to Dhoman with you—*none at all!*'

'If you wish to continue to exercise your mind, there

will be plenty that you can do to help me in Dhoman,'
he said quietly.

'Oh, for heaven's sake, Badyr—you haven't been
listening to a damn thing I've been saying!' she
exploded, pacing back and forth about the room.
Trying to calm down, she took a deep breath and
turned to face him. 'Surely . . . surely you could allow
us to remain here, in London?' she said as quietly and
as reasonably as she could. 'You must be so wealthy
now, that for you to fly over here to see Jade as often as
you like, would hardly make a dent in the petty cash!'

'But that is not what I want, Leonie. I have told you
that I wish my wife and daughter to live with me.'

'I'm sick and tired of hearing what *you* want!' Her
blue eyes flashed dangerously, regarding his casually
lounging figure with utter loathing. 'Why don't you get
yourself another wife? The world is full of women
who'd jump at the chance of marrying a real live
Sultan!'

Badyr shook his head. 'I want you,' he remarked
flatly.

'Why, for God's sake?'

'Maybe . . .' he hesitated. 'Maybe, because I wish to
have a son, hmm?'

'Don't be ridiculous! All you have to do is to find
another wife and possess yourself in patience for nine
months.' She gave a shrill laugh. 'As far as I'm
concerned, you can forget it! I'm *definitely* not prepared
to . . .'

'Enough!' Badyr rose slowly from the sofa, his deep
voice cutting abruptly through her breathless protest.
'As I promised, I have listened to what you have had to
say about the termination of our marriage. Nevertheless,
my mind remains unchanged. Both you and our child
will accompany me back to Dhoman immediately after
your mother's wedding. You are my wife, Leonie, and I
shall exercise a husband's rights, as and when I feel
inclined to do so. I am confident that with Allah's

blessing you will bear me many sons. There is nothing more to be said.'

Leonie gasped with outrage. 'I won't . . .'

'Oh, yes, you will.' He moved forward, placing a hand beneath her chin and tilting her face up towards him. 'It is foolish of you not to acknowledge that I hold all the cards in this affair.'

She stared up at the face so close to her own, her eyes filled with the grimly implacable, unrelenting expression on his harsh features. Badyr was right. He did hold all the cards. He knew, with absolute certainty, that she would never abandon her child.

'God—I hate you! I'll never forgive you for what you are doing to me,' she hissed through clenched teeth, unable to control the furious, impotent rage which was shaking her slim body. 'And . . . and both you and Allah will have to wait a bloody long time—because I'll never, *ever*, willingly submit to your so-called "husband's rights"!'

'No?' he whispered softly as he lowered his dark head, his mouth feathering tormentingly across her lips and reawakening the aching memory of just how she had once responded to his light caresses.

Her mouth was suddenly dry, her nerve ends screaming and every muscle tensed against his calculated, deliberate assault upon her senses. *She must get out of here!* Twisting away from Badyr's arms, she tried to control the involuntary trembling in her legs as she walked towards the door.

'Surely you cannot be leaving so soon, Leonie?' he drawled, his voice heavy with mockery. 'Have you forgotten that I wish you to dine with me tonight?'

She turned to face the tall, elegant figure who had caused her so much heartache in the past. He was so sure, so arrogantly confident of her capitulation, that it was all she could do not to scream with frustration.

'I have forgotten nothing—especially those dreadful few months of our marriage. And the thought of eating

dinner with you makes me feel sick!' she flung at him
bitterly. 'I'm going home now, and unless you intend to
use force and cause a scandal in this oh-so respectable
hotel, I suggest that there is damn-all you can do about
it.'

His figure stiffened, radiating a menacing force, and
for the first time that day Leonie sensed the unleashed
power of the anger her words had aroused, trembling at
the realisation of just how ruthless and dangerous this
man could be. And then he relaxed, smiling sardonically
as he picked up the phone and ordered his chauffeur-
driven Rolls to be brought around to the front door of
the hotel.

'Do not make the error of trying to escape, my dear
Leonie,' he warned her softly as she left the suite. 'I
have infinite resources at my command, and let there be
no doubt in your mind that when I return to Dhoman, I
shall most surely be accompanied by both you and my
daughter.'

Later that night as she lay in bed, staring blindly at the
ceiling, Badyr's taunting words ran like an evil refrain
through her tired mind. Driven back to her home in
solitary splendour, she had been filled with misery, her
only crumb of comfort being the contemplation of
exactly what she was going to say to her mother on her
return. But even there she had been frustrated, unable
to relieve her exacerbated feelings. The house had been
empty, with merely a note from her mother—the
coward!—explaining that she and Jade had gone to
have dinner and spend the night with old friends of the
family on the other side of London.

Leonie felt totally exhausted by the events of the day,
and yet the blessed relief of sleep evaded her. Try as she
might, she could find no avenue of escape from the
inevitability of her return to Dhoman. Even wild
schemes, such as escaping with Jade to some secret
destination, failed to stand up to more than a moment's

contemplation. Badyr had stated no more than the truth: with unlimited money and resources at his command, he would manage to track her down sooner or later. And then what? His anger at being defied would undoubtedly result in his immediate abduction of Jade. As ruler of his country, Badyr had absolute and total power over his subjects, and she knew that once her child had been taken to Dhoman, she would never see her again.

Dhoman! The very name of the place was enough to make her shudder. Ever since she had escaped from that country, she had done all she could to expunge the painful memories of her brief marriage. But now there seemed nothing she could do to prevent them from rising like ghosts from the past, powerless to stop the haunting nightmares from filling her mind to the exclusion of all else.

CHAPTER THREE

IT was now clear that her first meeting with Badyr, when Leonie had been so young and innocent, had been nothing but a disastrous, malign twist of fate. If only she hadn't been quite so anxious to prove her worth to her new employer, Dimitri Kashan, by exceeding her instructions and delivering a precious carpet to the wrong address and the wrong person—but she had and she did!

'No, I can assure you that I am *not* Mr Wilding!' The tall, outrageously handsome man had regarded her flustered face with amusement. 'However, I am sure this little matter can be easily sorted out. So, why not sit down and have a calming drink, while we consider what to do about the problem, hmm?'

Leonie had looked nervously around the luxurious sitting-room of the penthouse apartment, her mind filled with her mother's dire warnings about what happened to young girls who accepted drinks from strange men. Not realising that the expression on her lovely face, and the alarm reflected in her sapphire blue eyes had so clearly echoed her agitated thoughts, she had been startled when the man standing before her gave a short bark of laughter.

'I can assure you that you are quite safe!' His shoulders had shaken with amusement. 'You have my word of honour that I do not make a habit of seducing pretty young girls—even one as beautiful as you! So, let us be very correct and introduce ourselves, hmm?'

'I'm ... er ... Leonie Elliot,' she had murmured, staring fixedly down at the rolled-up rug she was carrying, and miserably aware of the deep flush staining her cheeks. This man must think that she was very silly and gauche. How she had longed to be a sophisticated woman of the world and able to make cool, clever conversation, instead of standing here tongue-tied and helplessly uncertain of what to do next.

'Very well, Leonie, you may call me Badyr,' the man had said, gently leading her stiff figure towards a soft leather chair. 'Now if you will make yourself comfortable, and give me that piece of paper containing what is clearly the wrong name and address, I'll see if we can't solve the mystery, hmm?'

He had left the room, Leonie hearing a short buzz of conversation before he returned with a tray containing tall glasses and a jug. 'I have asked my assistant to make enquiries and here, in the meantime, is a cool drink of orange juice—which I can promise you contains no wicked alcohol!'

Smiling shyly up at the man who was regarding her with a calm, friendly expression on his face, Leonie had found herself beginning to relax. It was really very kind of him to take so much trouble on her behalf, and she haltingly told him so.

'Think nothing of it, my dear Leonie,' he had grinned, sitting down on a wide sofa near her chair. 'It is clearly my duty to help a damsel in distress. Now,' he had added, filling her glass again, 'tell me all about yourself.'

'There's . . . well, there's really nothing much to tell,' she had begun, but under his skilful questioning she had soon found herself becoming more loquacious. It had been somehow very easy to talk to this man about just how much she missed her father and how, not knowing what she wanted to do on leaving school, she had been so grateful when an old friend of her father's, Dimitri Kashan, had offered her a job in his firm training to be an oriental rug broker. Since most of her school holidays had been spent in Iran, where rugmaking was an important part of the national economy, and where she had spent many hours visiting small village workshops watching the weavers at their looms, Leonie had jumped at the chance of working with such beautiful objects.

'Training to be an oriental rug broker is perhaps an unusual career? Especially for such a beautiful young girl, hmm?'

Leonie had been able to feel herself blushing, her heart beginning to beat in a hurried, nervous response to the increasing warmth in his voice. 'I . . . er . . . I'm not sure whether I'll still have a job after this mix-up with the carpet,' she had muttered unhappily. 'What on earth am I going to do?'

'What you are going to do, is to allow me to drive you home,' he had said firmly. 'I know Mr Kashan, and I can assure you that when I have spoken to him, there will be nothing for you to worry about.'

Leonie had spent a sleepless night wondering about what her employer would say, and also disturbed—not to say appalled—by the strange churning in her stomach, the hopeless longing and trembling excitement whenever she thought about Badyr. She had been sure that such a handsome, older man would have been bored by her youth and inexperience, and quite convinced that she would never see him again.

She had, therefore, been astounded when Dimitri Kashan had welcomed her the next morning with a beaming smile, and even more amazed to find that the man in the luxury apartment was a valued client of the firm. Prince Badyr of Dhoman, she learned, was the only son of a wealthy Arab sultan and had been brought up and educated in England. Her head had still been spinning when she returned home from work to find a huge bouquet of red roses awaiting her, together with a note from Badyr asking her to join him for dinner that night.

The next few weeks had been ones of halcyon enjoyment and happiness. A serving officer in the British Army, Badyr's regiment was based at Chelsea

Barracks in London, and he had insisted on seeing her every day, either taking her out to dinner or having a meal prepared by his Arab servants in his penthouse suite overlooking Hyde Park. Leonie had never tired of hearing about the past history of his country, Dhoman. She would sit curled up beside him on the sofa in his apartment as he told her how his country, situated at the foot of the Arabian peninsula overlooking the Arabian Sea, had once been a great sea-trading nation.

'People imagine that it is only a desert, but the south of the country is a wide, fertile green plain, once known as the Incense Coast because it provided the world with frankincense and other rare spices. Nowadays, our chief export is oil, although my father adamantly refuses to spend the revenues as he should—completely ignoring his people's dire need and poverty,' he had added bitterly.

That had been Leonie's first intimation of the strained relationship betwen father and son. Having sent Badyr to be educated in England, and encouraging him to take up a military career, Sultan Raschid had clearly not realised that such an education might well lead to his son taking a more democratic, liberal view of the responsibilities of a ruler.

'The days when one can run a country as if it was one's own private estate are dead and gone!' Badyr had exploded angrily as they returned to his apartment one evening. He had gone on to say that he had been given permanent leave of absence from his regiment, and he intended to return to Dhoman almost immediately.

'There has been constant trouble in the western part of my country for the past few years, mainly due to my father's dislike of all development—such as roads, hospitals and schools,' he had explained. 'Now, however, matters are becoming far more serious, and I have been informed by British army intelligence that both Russia and China are pouring arms into the area. I must go back and stand by my father's side, whether he wishes it or not. He needs me at such a time.'

Leonie had suddenly felt cold as ice, immobile as if she had been turned to stone. Ever since they had first met, Badyr's handsome image had seemed to haunt both her dreams and every waking moment, causing her to be so absent-minded that her employer, Dimitri Kashan, had been forced to protest: 'May the Good Lord preserve me from young girls in love!'

Was she in love? She had wondered how anyone knew if they were *really* in love? Leonie had only been aware that life had seemed to take on a new dimension when she was in Badyr's company, and without him she was somehow incomplete. However, since he had never attempted to do more than give her a chaste peck on her cheek as he delivered her back to her home each evening, she had had no idea of his feelings towards her.

Now, however, all doubts regarding her own emotions had been swept away. As a shaft of bitter agony pierced her heart, she had realised that she loved Badyr, and that she could not live without him. Gasping with pain, she had buried her face in her hands to hide the tide of desperate misery which racked her slim figure. A moment later she had felt his arms closing about her.

'Do not weep, my sweet Leonie,' he had murmured as she sobbed against his shoulder. 'Tell me what is wrong, hmm?'

'You are g-going away and . . . and I c-can't bear it. I love you s-so much . . .' she had stuttered, a deep blush spreading over her pale cheeks as she had realised just how she was betraying her feelings for him.

'Ah . . .' Badyr's tall frame had shaken as he gave a deep sigh. Lowering his head, his warm breath had fanned her flushed cheek as his lips had gently touched the corner of her trembling mouth in a soft, gentle caress. 'I too, my darling,' he had whispered. 'It is a very serious thing, is it not, for a man of my age to fall so completely in love—and with such a young girl?'

'*Oh, Badyr!*' she had exclaimed ecstatically, throwing her arms about his neck. 'I love you and . . .' The rest of her words had been lost as he had clasped her tighter, his mouth possessing hers with passionate intensity.

She had had no idea how long they stood locked together, but eventually his hold had slackened. 'I think that we had better sit down before I do something that we would both regret—like immediately taking you to my bed!' he had said hoarsely as he led her towards a sofa. 'I can see the headlines now,' he had grinned. ' "Arab man rapes young girl in Hyde Park apartment"—I somehow don't think your mother would approve!'

A hectic flush had swept over Leonie's cheeks. Although she had been strictly brought up, and had always concurred with the moral principle of chastity before marriage, for the first time in her life she had understood the driving force and power of sexual desire. Badyr had mentioned rape, but she had known that once she was clasped within his arms, she would have no other impulse but complete and total surrender to whatever he might demand of her. Emotionally excited and thrilled beyond words to find that he loved her, she had been so immersed in her own ecstatic thoughts that she had almost missed his next words.

'. . . as I intended. I had hoped that we could be married and spend many happy years together here in England, before I would be forced to take up my responsibilities in Dohman. But it is not to be. I cannot ask you to wait for me, neither can I expect you to accompany me to such a medieval, backward country, where life is so very different from that in England.'

'Oh, please! Please take me with you, Badyr,' she had begged. 'I . . . I'll die if you go away and leave me, I know I will!'

'Ah, my darling. When you look at me like that I am sorely tempted,' he had murmured thickly, gathering her slender body into his arms. 'I, too, cannot bear the

idea of life without you by my side. But you will find
the life so different, so restrictive, that I hesitate . . .'

'I love you so much,' she had told him earnestly. 'I
don't care what Dhoman's like, just as long as you and
I are together.'

Badyr had sighed heavily. 'How can I possibly resist
such a plea, since I too love you with all my heart? Very
well, my darling, it shall be as you say. I will ask your
mother for permission to marry you, and then we will
leave for Dhoman, together.'

'Oh, Badyr . . .! I'm . . . I'm *so* happy!' she had
murmured, tears of joy filling her eyes.

'I hope and pray that you may always be so,' he had
said quietly. The dark eyes gleaming down at her had
become shadowed, a troubled expression flickering
across his face for a moment, before he had smiled and
bent to kiss her soft lips. '*Insh'allah*, my beloved Leonie.
It shall be as God wills, hmm?'

They had been married a week later at the Regent's
Park Mosque, followed by a simple register office
wedding and a lavish reception afterwards at the Hyde
Park Hotel. Leonie had drifted through the day in a
hazy state of bliss, only truly aware of Badyr's tall
handsome figure, and her almost unbelievable joy at
being married to a man whom she loved with all her
heart.

It had taken a great deal of persuasion, on Badyr's
part, to gain Mrs Elliot's permission for the wedding to
go ahead. She had not been at all happy to learn that
her daughter was intent on marrying an Arab, and even
more disturbed to learn that the happy couple would be
going to live in a far-off and isolated part of Arabia.

'Not that I've got anything against Badyr, himself,'
her mother had said. 'He's a charming man, and I know
that he will always take the greatest care of you—his
assurances to me of his love and devotion were
genuinely touching and obviously sincere. But, darling,

you are so young—only eighteen!' She had frowned anxiously. 'And who has ever heard of Dhoman? Not only that—I'm told that Arab society is very, very different from anything we know in the West. It will be a totally strange way of life, and learning to live with someone else can be difficult enough, without adding cultural stresses and strains to the relationship.'

But Leonie had been adamant that their love for each other would surmount all obstacles, refusing to listen to any words of caution or the plea that she should wait a year before getting married, so as to be absolutely sure of her decision. And because she loved her daughter very dearly, Mrs Elliot had sighed and said no more.

Almost before she knew it, Leonie had said her emotional farewells, and was boarding the privately chartered aeroplane with her new husband, bound for a week's honeymoon in Paris before travelling on to Dhoman.

Leonie had never had any doubts about her physical response to Badyr, but his experienced lovemaking had been a revelation, an exquisite fulfilment that surpassed anything she could possibly have imagined. Knowing that she was a virgin, he had slowly and with infinite gentleness led her from one emotional delight to another. Beneath his skilful expertise, as his mouth and hands savoured every inch of her slender, quivering body, she had begun to comprehend the true meaning of emotional ecstasy. Eagerly welcoming both the pain and then the pulsating pleasure of his hungry possession, her conscious self had become submerged in a raging storm of desire as he raised her, emotionally and physically, to the very peak of passionate sensuality.

Day after day and night after night, Badyr had clearly demonstrated his inexhaustible desire for her body. Under his masterly tuition, she had learned to finally discard all her virginal inhibitions, wantonly responding to the piercing sweetness of his lips, wildly and passionately returning his intimate caresses.

But all too soon, it seemed, their idyll was over. Badyr had arranged that they would break their journey at Abu Dhabi, spending a night with his father's youngest sister, who had married a member of Abu Dhabi's ruling family.

It had been Leonie's first real glimpse of Arabia, and she had found it disconcerting. From the modern, futuristic design of the airport building which looked like a giant, psychedelic mushroom, to the shimmering glass-towered office blocks surrounded by shady parks and gardens overflowing with tropical blooms in riotous colours, it had seemed light-years away from her previous notions of what constituted a desert city.

Later that evening as Leonie had stood on the open balcony of their palatial bedroom, she had felt the first stirrings of apprehension and unease. Badyr's aunt couldn't have been kinder to her. A small, bustling woman, she had kissed Leonie enthusiastically on the cheek and seen to the girl's every comfort. However, it had quickly become apparent to them both that Leonie hadn't the faintest notion about the traditional customs or what was expected of women in Arabia. She hadn't known, for instance, that it wasn't usual for men and women to eat together—even husbands and wives having separate meals with members of their own sex. Nor had she been very successful at disguising her shock at having to wear a black veil covering her face when strange visitors called. She had also been clearly bewildered by the fact that among the guests at the aunt's female-only dinner-party—all of whom seemed to be clothed in dresses from the top Parisian fashion houses, and wearing magnificent jewellery the like of which she had never seen before—most of the women did not use a fork, but scooped up the food with the fingers of their right hand. Trying to teach Leonie to eat the same way, the women had screamed with laughter both at her awkwardness and the resulting mess on her clothes.

'I must have a long talk to Badyr as soon as possible!' his aunt had exclaimed in some agitation at the depth of the English girl's ignorance. 'How much has he told you about my brother, the Sultan, and the life that you will be expected to live in Dhoman?'

'Nothing, really,' Leonie had murmured, feeling tired and exhausted by all the cultural shocks of the day.

'I see,' the older woman had frowned. 'Well, if we have time before you leave tomorrow, I will try to tell you all I can.'

Which was very kind of her, Leonie reflected, unable to repress a shiver even though there was no breeze to disturb the hot night air. She had been so immersed in her thoughts that she had not heard Badyr's approach, giving a start of surprise as she felt his arms go about her slim waist.

'I must talk to you,' she had begun. 'I didn't realise ... I mean, it's all so very ...'

'Come to bed, my beloved,' Badyr had whispered, burying his face in the fragrant cloud of her red-gold hair.

'Please, Badyr, I'm worried, and ...'

'Tomorrow. We will talk about what worries you tomorrow, hmm? Just now, I am far more interested in other matters!' His eyes gleamed in the darkness as he had turned her to face him, his mouth coming down to possess her lips in a warm, lingering kiss. 'Ah, my darling, I fear I am insatiably addicted to your delicious body,' he had breathed huskily, his hands moving slowly and sensually over the full curves of her breasts. As she had gasped and trembled at his touch, he had given a soft, low laugh, sweeping her up in his arms and moving swiftly over to the bed, where his vigorous, erotic lovemaking had quickly banished everything from her mind, save the driving need to ardently respond to the passion that flared between them.

Waking late the next morning, she had dressed and gone downstairs, drawn to the sound of voices coming from an open door. Standing in the doorway, she had been startled to see the small figure of his aunt, angrily yelling at Badyr who stood rigidly silent, growing pale as the tirade continued. Leonie had thought she heard her name mentioned once or twice, but it was impossible to be sure among the stream of incomprehensible language issuing from the mouth of the small, furious woman.

Badyr had gestured towards Leonie, and his aunt had fallen silent for a moment. 'Well,' she had sighed, speaking in English, 'I have done what I can. No one can say that you haven't been warned. But I do beg you to be careful, Badyr, because the situation is now very, very dangerous.'

'What's dangerous?' Leonie had asked, feeling suddenly frightened by the serious note in the older woman's voice.

'Nothing that need concern you,' Badyr had replied curtly. His dismissive words were clearly nonsense, and Leonie could feel her hackles rise at being treated like a child. However, his aunt was loudly clapping her hands for coffee, and it had proved impossible to pursue the matter any further.

There had been little time before they left Abu Dhabi for Badyr's aunt to do more than show Leonie how to wear the *abaya*, the black covering worn by Arab women outside their home. That, and her whispered injunction, when Badyr left the room for a moment, to contact the older woman if there should be trouble of any kind, had left Leonie in a state of apprehensive confusion. Badyr had not chosen to give a sensible answer to any of her questions during the flight to Dhoman, and so she had been totally ignorant of what lay ahead as their small plane prepared to land, circling over a mountain range in front of which lay the sandy plain and deep blue sea of her future homeland.

They had been met at the airport by one of the most ancient-looking cars she had ever seen. Wheezing and gasping as if at its last breath, it had moved slowly along a winding road behind their official escort—an equally old Landrover—which had raised such a cloud of blinding dust that it wasn't until Badyr tapped her on the shoulder that she had realised that they had arrived at the Sultan's palace.

Peering out of the car's dusty window, she had been amazed and struck speechless by the sheer size of the mammoth, grey stone fortress-like building, hardly able to believe that this was where she was going to live. Built in the sixteenth century by the Portuguese to guard the entrance to the port of Muria, the capital of Dhoman, it was still heavily dominating the old walled city all these hundreds of years later.

Later that evening, as she and Badyr were changing their clothes prior to the first official meeting with the Sultan, Leonie had shivered as she gazed at her surroundings. Despite the heat, the stark grey stone walls gave off an unpleasant, clammy chill—accurately reflecting the frigidly cold welcome to her son's wife extended by Badyr's mother, the Sultana Zenobia. The only cheerful face had been that of his sister, Maryam, a pretty young girl of fourteen, who had given Leonie a shy smile of welcome.

When she and Badyr had walked through the great Moorish arch into the castle—the heavy wooden door thundering ominously as it was closed firmly behind them—he had mentioned that his father, the Sultan, had his own private apartments, and that they would be living with his mother whose large, private quarters were known as the Harem.

Leonie had felt inclined to giggle at first hearing of such an archaic arrangement, far more reminiscent of the Caliphs of Baghdad than the modern-day world! However, after what little she had seen of the palace, all desire to laugh had abruptly vanished. As for Badyr's mother—while clearly doting on her son, the older woman had made it instantly and quite unmistakably obvious that she did not approve of his marriage.

Later that evening, Leonie had still been trying to dismiss the lump of depression in her stomach and think positively about her situation. It hadn't been easy. As she had wandered disconsolately through the suite of rooms which had been allocated to them, she had shivered at the sight of the dank walls, bare of any ornament or decoration. All this place needed to make it a real home from home, she had thought almost hysterically, was a rack and some thumbscrews! Defiantly humming a tune under her breath in a vain attempt to try and keep up her spirits, she had slowly retraced her steps into the bedroom

Pausing on the threshold, her eyes had widened as she gazed at her husband. Badyr had finished dressing, his tall figure clothed in a simple, long white robe, edged about the neck and down the front by bands of gold thread. A large, curved ceremonial dagger, whose hilt and scabbard were made from heavily engraved solid gold, had been plunged through the front of the thick, wide gold belt clasping his slim waist; the only splash of colour being the length of shimmering multi-coloured silk wound intricately about his head to form a turban, the fringed end of which rested on his left shoulder.

Watching as he slipped on a flowing white silk cloak, edged like his robe with thick bands of gold, Leonie had blinked her eyes several times in an effort to clear her stunned mind. Talk about the Sheikh of Araby! Badyr had looked . . . well, there was no doubt that he looked *absolutely sensational!*

Unfortunately, it had seemed that Badyr took a less than enthusiastic view of her own apparel. His mouth had tightened with annoyance as he viewed the low-cut bodice of a long, sapphire-blue chiffon dress, supported by thin strips of satin tied in a bow on her bare shoulders.

'*Wallahi—Leonie!* You can't possibly wear that!' he had exclaimed in a harsh, rough voice. 'Don't you realise that my father would have a fit if he saw you in that creation? You must wear a dress that has long sleeves and which completely covers all your flesh. Surely you have such a garment?'

'In this climate? Are you crazy? Of course I haven't!' she had snapped. It had been a long, tiring day and she had felt as if she was going to burst into tears at any moment.

Badyr had taken no notice of her outburst, striding over to the heavily carved wardrobe, the only piece of furniture in the room other than the huge bed, to look swiftly through her clothes.

'You are right, there is nothing here that is suitable,' he had muttered. 'However—yes, this will do.'

'That . . .? But . . . but it's only something to wear on the beach!' Leonie had looked with dismay at the plain black, flimsy garment. Made from fine lawn and cut in the shape of a caftan, it might be just the thing to wear over a swimsuit, but there had been no way it was going to be suitable for this evening's reception.

'Beach—what beach?' Badyr had given a harsh, sardonic laugh. 'Where do you think we are, the South of France? Surely you can't have been so foolish as to imagine that you will be allowed to sunbathe or go swimming, here in Dhoman?'

'But I thought . . .'

'You're not expected to think, Leonie!' he had snapped curtly. 'Just do as you're told, and put that dress on as quickly as possible. My father is a great stickler for punctuality and will be furious if we are late.'

She had been much too shocked by the sudden and completely unexpected change in her husband's personality to do more than snatch the material from his hands and run blindly towards the bathroom. How could Badyr, who had always been so kind and gentle,

talk to her in that harsh, caustic tone? And why she had
to wear this caftan, she had had absolutely no idea.
Wiping the tears of self-pity from her eyes, she had
contemplated the black sack-like dress with distaste.

'Well, I hope you're satisfied!' she had grumbled, as
she had walked slowly back into the bedroom. 'As far
as I'm concerned, I think I look simply awful.'

'We have no time to worry about how you feel, it is
far more important not to keep my father waiting,' he
had retorted sternly, taking her hand and leading her
swiftly from the room.

Her first meeting with the Sultan had proved to be
something of an ordeal. A small thin man, he had
slowly entered the large room where she and Badyr,
together with his mother and sister, were waiting.
Moving in majestic silence towards a low throne, he
had completely ignored his wife, his daughter and the
son whom he hadn't seen for some years, as he
beckoned Leonie over to sit on the carpet beside him.
She hadn't known what to do, so she had remained
sitting quietly, peering up cautiously through her
eyelashes at the austere, melancholic expression on his
face.

After an interminable silence, he had turned towards
her, his large dark eyes almost sleepy-looking beneath
their heavy eyelids, and politely asked if she had
enjoyed her journey, and was there anything that she
required?

Leonie had been struck dumb, completely nonplussed
by his question, which had been spoken in perfect
English. What on earth was she supposed to say? A
quick glance at Badyr's stern face had given her no
assistance, although his dark eyes seemed to be trying
to tell her something. But what? She had hesitated and
then, remembering how she hadn't been able to
understand a word of the argument between Badyr and
his aunt, she had asked if she could have a tutor to help
her to learn Arabic.

The sudden, electrifying tension which swept through the room as she voiced her simple request had been very frightening. Nobody had moved, nobody had spoken a word, yet all the members of his family had seemed to be waiting with bated breath for the reaction of Sultan Raschid.

'Hmm,' he had murmured, after a lengthy pause. 'I do not normally believe in education, and especially not for women, of course!' he had added, giving her a wintry smile. 'Perhaps you are not aware of the interesting fact, but it is precisely because the British were so foolish as to educate the masses in India, that they lost their empire.'

The Sultan had seemed to be expecting an answer. 'No, I ... didn't know that,' she had mumbled, wishing that she had never opened her mouth. There was no doubt that Badyr's father was a very peculiar old man, but this was clearly neither the time, or indeed the place, to publicly disagree with his nonsensical statement about education in the Indian sub-continent.

'However, learning to speak our ancient language is something of which I am prepared to approve,' Sultan Raschid had said, after another long silence. 'It shall be arranged.' He had stood up. 'I will now retire and hold a private conversation with my son.'

Surprised and bewildered by the palpable sighs of relief with which the Sultan's pronouncement had been received, Leonie had scrambled to her feet on legs which felt numb; it had been obvious that sitting on a hard floor for any length of time was an art she had yet to acquire. By the time she had risen, the Sultan had whisked himself out of the room, with Badyr moving swiftly in his wake. Looking around, she had been disconcerted to receive an ice-cold glare of dislike from Sultana Zenobia, before she had spoken sharply to her young daughter. Maryam, who seemed the only normal person in the extraordinary palace set-up, had smiled and given Leonie a friendly wink, before she hurried away from her mother.

Left totally on her own, Leonie had had no idea what she was supposed to do. After many false turnings and getting completely lost once or twice, she had found her own suite of rooms. Sitting all alone for what seemed liked eternity, she had eventually taken off her dress and crawled miserably into bed. There had been no sign of Badyr, and she had finally drifted off to sleep, her cheeks damp with unhappy tears.

That first evening at the palace in Dhoman had been a precursor of all that was to follow: long periods of silent loneliness, interrupted by occasional meetings with the Sultan, who had surprised everyone by taking a considerable interest in his son's new wife. Other than copies of the Koran—printed in Arabic, of course— there had been no books in the palace, and since Leonie had omitted to bring any reading material with her to Dhoman, she had frequently given thanks to whatever had prompted her request for tuition in Arabic. She had been convinced that without the daily lessons she would have gone stark, staring mad.

Badyr's mother, Zenobia, had made life in the palace as uncomfortable for her son's wife as she possibly could, never letting up on what Leonie came to see as the older woman's relentless, guerrilla warfare. Meal times would be suddenly and unexpectedly altered for no reason, and more often than not Leonie would go downstairs to find that all the food had been eaten. After a while it had seemed easier to arrange for her personal servant, Hussa, to bring the food to her rooms—thus increasing her lonely isolation.

The main pinprick, until Leonie began to master the intricacies of the extremely difficult language, had been her mother-in-law's refusal to speak to her in anything but Arabic, although Leonie knew from Maryam that the older woman possessed a good command of English. The servants, of course, only spoke in their own language, and she had been reduced to spending hours acting out the simplest requests, which often resulted in tears of frustration on her part unless she could find Maryam and gain her assistance.

It had been Maryam, a bright and amusing fourteen-year-old, who had helped Leonie to retain her sanity. It had seemed that there was nothing the young girl didn't know about what was going on in the palace, and also in the country at large. It had been through Maryam that she had first come to know that the Sultan had another wife, the Sultana Fatima, and two other young daughters who lived in a far wing of the palace.

'Mother and Fatima get on very well. Fatima's so fat and lazy that she always agrees with everything Mother says,' Maryam had grinned. 'However, the most important aid to their friendship is that Fatima hasn't produced a son, who might have threatened Badyr's chance of succeeding my father as Sultan. That's been my mother's greatest fear. She didn't want Badyr to come back here,' Maryam had added with a worried frown. 'Not when father's so ... well, so odd—if you know what I mean?'

Leonie had known exactly what she meant. Sultan Raschid, who at first sight had seemed to be such a benign, if somewhat peculiar old man, had turned out to be not only odd and eccentric, but a man of whom his wife, Zenobia, was clearly terrified. When Leonie had seen that hard, tough and ambitious woman quailing with fear in his presence, she had recalled the words of Badyr's aunt in Abu Dhabi. Had it been Sultan Raschid to whom she had referred as 'very dangerous'?

The edicts issued by the Sultan: banning such items as sunglasses, the live playing of music and radios, cigarettes, dancing, all travel between towns without a permit, and even the wearing of trousers by men, had been irritating but relatively harmless. However, it was his fierce, obdurate refusal to spend any of his vast oil revenues on important and necessary items such as schooling or medicine that had led to the present unrest and rebellion in the western part of the country. There were, apparently, only three small primary schools in the whole of Dhoman, and no hospitals or health service other than that offered by a small clinic in Muria, run by a dedicated group of American doctors.

Outside the Sultan's palace, his subjects were living a life of unrelieved hardship, their dire poverty compounded by the dreadful conditions in which they lived. Malaria was rife, tuberculosis and trachoma—that dreadful, blinding disease of the eyes—were chronic conditions which affected most of the inhabitants.

Inside the palace, the old grey walls almost shook and trembled with the ferocity of the daily rows between father and son. Badyr, who was growing increasingly tense and angry at his inability to persuade the Sultan to distribute some of his wealth among his people, had told her that the infant mortality was among the highest in the world.

'No wonder my father doesn't bother to build any more schools,' he had raged one evening when they were alone in the privacy of their suite. 'Judging by the way the poor, tragic little babies are dying, there will be no need for more school places. Is it any wonder that many of our people are beginning to listen to Marxist propaganda? Who can blame them for seeking to overthrow my father's unjust, uncaring rule?'

Quite apart from her imprisonment within the harem quarters of the palace, and the deliberate unkindness of Sultana Zenobia, Leonie's difficulties had been compounded by the fact that Badyr was so often absent. He rose early, and only returned to their rooms in the palace late at night. She had no idea where he went or whom he saw, since he categorically refused to discuss the matter. It had only been from Maryam that she learnt of his secret talks with some of the influential tribal Sheikhs, and even more secret meetings with members of the Sultan's army and air force.

Increasingly, it had seemed as if the only moments she and Badyr shared together were those when he slid silently into bed at night, often waking her from an uneasy sleep as he sought the comfort of her arms. As the weeks had passed by, his lovemaking became more intense and more strained. It had been as though he wasn't making love to *her* any more, but somehow trying to exorcise his increasing frustration and anger with his father, by demonstrating his ruthless dominance of her body.

She had tried very hard to be understanding. She had known how frustrated Badyr was by his father's obstinate refusal to discuss the affairs of the country, and she had realised that his position was becoming even more untenable than her own. But there appeared to be little she could do to prevent herself from becoming increasingly resentful, both of the way he had virtually abandoned her in this vast palace, and his use of her body to gain physical and emotional relief.

Being able to wear a king's ransom in jewellery, and clothed in the rich silk and satin gowns given to her by Badyr, meant nothing—not when compared to the loss of her liberty and the increasing tension between them. Eventually, of course, she had rebelled; rejecting his approaches and refusing to respond to his demands. And it had been then that their relationship quickly disintegrated into what seemed a war of attrition. Badyr had no longer whispered soft, sweet, tender words of love. With savage, bitter determination he had broken through the barriers she tried to erect between them, and using all the sexual mastery at his command he had aroused her weak flesh until she had been helpless, unable to do anything but respond feverishly to his lovemaking; her eyes filling with tears of shame and humiliation as night after night he had cruelly demonstrated her physical weakness.

'We can't go on like this, Badyr—we simply can't!' she had cried hopelessly one evening, impotently beating her fists against the hard body pinning her to the bed.

'Why not?' he had demanded with bitter ferocity. 'Your body is crying out for my touch!'

'No . . .!'

'You lie,' he had grated thickly, grasping her wrists and pinning them above her head. 'I'm an experienced man, Leonie, and I *know* when a woman is crazy with desire for me,' he had added cruelly.

He had been right, Leonie admitted to herself later, writhing with self-contempt. There had seemed to be nothing she could do to prevent herself from submitting to his demands. He had only to look at her and she trembled with desire, her flesh melting at his slightest touch.

Despite her pleas, he had made love to her that night with a desperate intensity that far surpassed anything she had experienced before. It was as if he was demanding not only her submission to his bodily needs, but her total subjection to his will, withholding complete satisfaction until she begged and pleaded for mercy. The passion that exploded between them following her moaning, abject capitulation had been savage and brutal, leaving Leonie to mourn the final nail in the coffin of all her hopes and dreams; weeping for the loss of warm, tender love as she found herself trapped in the dark forces of a living hell.

It couldn't go on, of course. He was destroying every shred of her pride and self-respect, and so lonely and desperate had she become that she knew she must escape from both Badyr and Dhoman. She had had no idea how she was going to manage such a task, but in the event matters were taken out of her hands. After a final, terrible argument with his father, Badyr had suddenly been placed under arrest. He had requested and been granted five minutes with his wife, and Leonie had been taken to a small room where Badyr, looking pale and strained, quickly took her into his arms.

'My beloved, I have no time to say anything, but to beg you to forgive me, and to remember that I love you,' he had whispered urgently as they both tried to ignore the guards at the door. 'Be calm and very, *very* careful of my father. Always present to him a smiling face, whatever you might feel in your heart. And always remember that I will return—you may be very sure of that. When that day comes, we shall begin our marriage again, hmm?'

Her eyes had been blind with tears as he was marched away, and it wasn't until some days later that she had learned that Badyr was under house arrest in one of the Sultan's palaces, far away in the south of Dhoman. Her terror for his safety had been compounded by the news which filtered through into the Harem, that one of his uncles had mysteriously disappeared, immediately after protesting about Badyr's arrest.

The removal of her son seemed to have aged Sultana Zenobia overnight. She had no longer bothered to make life difficult for Leonie, but stayed hidden away in her rooms, seeing no one. The silent, gloomy palace had been filled with whispers about the flood of people leaving the country, especially the young sons of the ruling sheikhs, and the daily rumours of sudden arrests and executions had led to an atmosphere of ever-increasing fright and terror. Apart from her own desperate worries, Leonie had been distressed to see Maryam's bright personality dimmed by the menace and tension which seemed to ooze from the very walls of the fortress. Leonie had encouraged the young girl to spend more of her time in the warm, comfortable quarters of Fatima, the Sultan's second wife. There, with her half-sisters, Nadia and Sara, she could escape from the unpredictable rages to which her father was becoming increasingly prone. In fact, it had been Leonie who was most often called upon to bear the

brunt of these tirades. It was as if the old man was
using her to continue the arguments with his son, now
imprisoned so far away in the south of the country.

It wasn't until a month after Badyr's sudden arrest,
when she had found herself feeling sick and dizzy in the
mornings, that Leonie had realised that she must be
pregnant. Almost collapsing with despair and loneliness,
she had rallied her forces enough to swear Hussa to
absolute secrecy, and had waited for an opportunity to
ask the Sultan if she could join Badyr in his captivity.
Although they had been so miserable together in the old
palace, maybe the knowledge that she was going to bear
his child would help them to overcome their past
difficulties? And no prison could be worse than the
strain of having to face the Sultan as he harangued and
shouted at her, night after night.

When Leonie had finally summoned up the courage
to make her request, Badyr's father had replied by
laughing in her face.

'Oh, no! Oh, dear me no, my pretty one,' he had
cackled with mirth. 'Why do you think I continue to
keep you here under my eye, eh? Haven't you realised
that you are the surety for my son's good behaviour?
He has been told that I will consign you to a
dungeon if he even talks to anyone, let alone attempts
to escape!'

Leonie had watched in horror as wild laughter shook
the old man's thin frame, his head nodding and jerking
with maniacal glee at the cleverness of his evil
stratagem.

Shaking with tension as she made her way back to
her lonely suite of rooms, Leonie had thrown herself
down on the bed in despair. She now knew that she had
no alternative but to escape from the palace—and
Dhoman—if she and her unborn child were to survive.
She had grown desperate as three more terrifying weeks
had dragged by and then, just as she had almost given
up hope, she had been summoned to Sultana Zenobia's

presence, where she had been astounded to hear the older woman address her in English for the first time.

'Allah knows I wished to have nothing further to do with you, but it now seems I have no alternative. How could Badyr have been so foolish as to have married you? A foreign woman!' she had snarled venomously. 'Oh, yes. It is entirely your fault that my son has been banished.'

'That ... that's not true!' Leonie had protested. 'It's the Sultan. He's mad—completely deranged! You, of all people, must know that.'

Zenobia had blanched as Leonie's passionate outburst rang around the room. 'Be quiet, you fool, these walls have ears!' she had hissed, glancing quickly over her shoulder. 'Guard your tongue, or I will never gain my son's release.'

'Can ... can you really help Badyr to escape?' Leonie had breathed, hope leaping in her heart at the older woman's words.

'Eventually, yes. However, none of my plans can be put into action—until you leave our country. Therefore your departure from Dhoman must be arranged as soon as possible. Unless ...' Zenobia had paused, her dark eyes narrowing as she stared at the trembling figure of the pale English girl. 'Can it be that you are expecting a child?'

'No—no, of course not!' Leonie had lied quickly, certain that if she told the truth she would be forced to remain in the palace for ever.

'That is good,' the older woman had nodded to herself. 'Very well, you may go,' she had waved dismissively. 'You will be contacted soon.'

Anxiously waiting, Leonie had almost given up hope when Hussa had woken her one night. Cautioning silence, the servant had led her through one winding passage after another, until they had reached a small wooden door set in the outer wall of the fortress. Releasing the rusty bolts, Hussa had begged Leonie to

hurry, leading the way through the silent streets to the
waterfront. From there Leonie had been taken on board a
dhow, and hidden among a pile of oriental rugs and
carpets. Violently sea-sick, she had no idea of the
length of the voyage, the fishing-boat eventually
delivering her and the rugs to Badyr's aunt in Abu Dhabi,
where she had been fed and clothed and put on a plane to
London. His aunt had insisted that she keep the carpets,
which she had subsequently sold to Dimitri Kashan. The
money from their sale, and her old job he had offered her
back after Jade's birth, had released her from all financial
worries, leaving only the torture of her constant heartache
for Badyr to burden those first years after her return.

Even after the birth of Jade, she had clung to Badyr's
promise of a happy future together—continuing to have
faith in his words. However, when she read reports in
the newspapers of the coup and his assumption of
power in Dhoman—and had still not heard a word
from him well over a year later—she had realised that
their marriage was over. During the years that followed,
she had finally accepted the brutal truth that Badyr had
never really loved her. She saw that her patent
adoration, coming as it did at a time of great stress in
his life, had merely been a salve to soothe and assuage
his anguish over the future of his country.

It had been a hard lesson, but she had learnt it well.
The experience had left such a scar on her mind and
body, that Leonie had determined never to become
emotionally involved again, concentrating all her energy
on her job and her little daughter. Now, with Badyr's
sudden reappearance, the carefully constructed edifice
of her new life lay in ruins about her.

God knew how she was going to endure living in that
dreadful country, but for Jade's sake, she had no
alternative but to return. Gasping with pain at the
thought of her future lonely existence, Leonie rolled over
to bury her head in the pillows, her slender body racked
by deep sobs of bitter, wretched misery and desolation.

CHAPTER FOUR

LEONIE slept fitfully, tossing and turning in the night, her mind and body racked by painful recollections. Waking early, and feeling far too agitated to even think of trying to go back to sleep, she slipped into a warm dressing-gown and padded downstairs in search of a soothing cup of tea. The silence of the empty house felt strange and lonely without Jade's bright morning chatter—providing confirmation that she had taken the right decision last night. The thought of returning to Dhoman with Badyr was almost unbearable, but she had no doubts at all that to have risked losing her little daughter would have been a totally unacceptable alternative.

The realisation that she had chosen the lesser of two evils proved of little comfort to her sorely tried nerves. The aspirins she had taken for the headache that throbbed and pounded in her head didn't seem to be working at all, and she was still feeling like death warmed up when Mrs Elliot returned to the house an hour later.

'Hello, darling. Shouldn't you be at work? I've just dropped Jade off at her playschool, but goodness, the traffic—it gets worse every day . . .'

'Okay—you can relax, Mother!' Leonie snapped, her voice cutting ruthlessly across the older woman's breathless stream of words. 'There's no need to pretend that you didn't know Badyr was intending to meet me last night, because your precious son-in-law has already spilt the beans. I understand that it's all thanks to you, that the dreadful man has come back into my life— *thanks a bunch!*' she ground out through clenched teeth.

Her mother gave her a quick, nervous glance.

'Now, darling, there's no need to be so upset. I knew you'd be cross, but . . .'

'Cross . . .! I'm not cross, for heaven's sake—*I'm bloody livid!*' she shouted, before wincing as the sound echoed in her aching head. 'How could you do it to me? That's what I don't understand. You know what a state I was in when I managed to escape from that ghastly country. So, how can you possibly have conspired and . . . and plotted behind my back with Badyr to make me go back to Dhoman?

'That's not fair!' Mrs Elliot protested sharply. 'I certainly didn't "conspire", as you put it, but I have been very worried about you and Jade. What's going to happen to you both after I'm married to Clifford, and living far away in Florida?'

'For heaven's sake! I've told you that we'll be fine.'

'You haven't managed to find anyone to look after her, have you? And what sort of life is it, being left all day with a complete stranger?'

'Oh—stuff and nonsense!' Leonie retorted. 'Thousands of women go out to work, and their children are perfectly all right. In any case, she'll soon be five and going to school all day—so that particular argument doesn't hold much water, does it?'

Her mother's mouth tightened into a stubborn line. 'Jade still needs her father. I knew you wouldn't like it, so I didn't tell you that I'd been in touch with Badyr during the last year. I never mentioned anything about you,' she assured her daughter earnestly. 'Only sending him photographs and information about Jade—she is his child, after all. I've made no secret of the fact that I've always thought it very, very wrong of you to keep all news of her from him. Can't you try and think about Jade and not yourself, just for once?'

Leonie gave a deep, unhappy sigh. 'Oh, Mother, you simply don't understand, do you?' she said, burying her face in her hands for a moment. 'How can I convince you that Dhoman isn't anything like a normal Arab state? It . . . it's going to be like going right back into the Middle Ages! Jade and I will be trapped in a harem, never going anywhere or seeing anyone.'

'Badyr assures me all that has changed,' her mother interjected quickly. 'He told me that he has never ceased to love you, and that your life will be quite different from what it was under his father's regime. He's built a new palace for you, and there are now schools and hospitals and . . .'

' "Never ceased to love me"? *Hah!*' Leonie snorted in derision. 'How can you believe such rubbish? Did the swine also tell you that he had every intention of snatching Jade away from me, if I didn't agree to go back?' Her voice wobbled as she fought back the tears. 'Were you really part of that blackmail plot?'

'*No!*' Mrs Elliot looked at her with shocked eyes. 'I can't believe that he could possibly . . .'

'Oh, yes—he threatened to do just that! And you thought he was such a reasonable man, such a charming son-in-law?' she laughed wildly. 'Well, I could have told you that you needed a very long spoon when you dined with that particular devil!'

'Oh, darling, I never thought . . .'

Leonie sighed again and wearily shrugged her shoulders. 'There's no point in my going on about it, is there? How could I let him abduct Jade—to have her taken away and never to see her again? So, I have no choice but to agree to give up my job and return to Dhoman, do I? Apparently we're scheduled to leave right after your wedding—*isn't that nice?*'

Mrs Elliot flinched at the bitter, caustic tone in her daughter's voice. 'What are you going to do?' she muttered, hurrying after Leonie as she walked away into the hall. 'I can always phone Clifford and postpone the wedding.'

'Absolutely not!' Leonie said, slipping on her overcoat. 'There's no point in mucking up two lots of lives. You and Clifford really love each other, and I'll be furious if you two don't settle down and live happily ever after. As for me? Well, I shouldn't have married Badyr in the first place, should I? I wouldn't listen to any good advice then, so I've got no one but myself to blame for having got into such a mess.'

'But where are you going?' her mother asked anxiously.

'I'm going to phone the office and tell them that I won't be in today, and then I must see Dimitri Kashan to give him my resignation in person—it's the least I can do after all his kindness. After which ... I'm intending to have a quiet walk in the park until it's time to pick Jade up from playschool. But don't panic! I'm not going to drown myself in the Round Pond—if that's what's worrying you,' she added wryly, and then immediately felt ashamed of herself as Mrs Elliot's face blanched at her words.

'I'm sorry, Mother,' she sighed heavily. 'I suppose you only did what you thought was best for us all, and with the very best intentions.' She bent forward to kiss the older woman's cheek. 'I ... well, I'm just so upset that I can't seem to think straight at the moment, I'm afraid.'

'What are you going to do about telling Jade?'

'I don't know, that's one of the things I'll have to think about,' Leonie muttered as she picked up the phone.

Gwen, her secretary, was calm and reassuring, confirming that there were no clients requiring her immediate attention, and that any letters or paperwork could easily wait until tomorrow.

Leonie had been dreading the interview with her employer, but in the event the old man had been kindness itself.

'There is no need to worry, Leonie. I am much better and can easily come back to work next week—I have been itching to do so, in any case!' he laughed. 'Well, well, so you are going back to Dhoman, eh? It is, of course, quite understandable that your husband should wish you to return, hmm?'

His keen old eyes searched the girl's face. There was clearly more to this affair than was apparent on the surface. The story she had given him—of a sudden reconciliation with her husband—did not exactly ring true. Not when he was well aware that the couple had not seen or communicated with each other for the past five years.

'However, my dear Leonie,' he continued, 'if ever the need should arise, do not hesitate to come and see me. And you may rest assured that your old job will always be waiting here for you.'

Later that morning as she walked slowly through Kensington Gardens, her boots scrunching over the skeletons of dead leaves, her mind seemed to be bursting with all the things she had to do, all the arrangements that must be made in the short time allotted to her by Badyr. It wasn't just a matter of clothes for herself and Jade, it also meant remembering to pack all the hundred and one everyday items which had been completely unobtainable in Dhoman. Locked up inside the Harem, she could well recall the frustrating difficulty in even trying to obtain such a simple thing as a toothbrush.

With a heavy sigh, she sat down on a park bench, stuffing her cold hands deep into the pockets of her coat and trying to impose some sort of order on the chaotic thoughts racing through her brain. Badyr had assured her mother that everything was now changed in Dhoman, but she couldn't believe that he had been able to alter such a system—a way of life which had been in existence for hundreds of years. She could remember, only too well, the stupefying boredom, the hours and hours of what amounted to solitary confinement, and the ever-increasing strain between Badyr and herself.

The past was past, she told herself firmly, thrusting aside the bitter memories. Of far more immediate importance was the necessity to tell Jade that Badyr was now here, in London, and that in under two weeks they would be returning with him to Dhoman.

Leonie had always taken the greatest care to see that her daughter knew she had a father—just like other little girls. She had also tried to stress the point that if he wasn't living with them, it was only because he couldn't leave his country, so far away on the other side of the world. Leonie knew that this simple explanation, first voiced when she still believed that Badyr would eventually get in touch with her, wouldn't satisfy Jade for very long. Although only four years old, the child was bright, very intelligent and already beginning to ask some awkward questions. Such as: why didn't her daddy get on an aeroplane to come over and see her? And: if he couldn't leave his country, wouldn't it be a good idea if she and her mummy went to see him? Leonie had fielded those very reasonable enquiries as best she could, but now the crunch had come, and she had no idea of how Jade would react to Badyr's sudden arrival. Nor, for that matter, how he was likely to view the daughter he had never seen.

Leonie's mouth curved into an ironic smile at the thought of her husband trying to cope with Jade's boisterous spirits, her non-stop chatter and the interminable questions. If he thought that he was due to meet a sweet, demure little girl—well, he was certainly going to be in for a surprise!

Glancing down at her watch, she gave a small yelp of dismay. She must stop day-dreaming here in the park and hurry back to the car, otherwise she would be late in picking up Jade from her playschool.

When they returned home, it was to find Mrs Elliot in a thoroughly flustered state.

'Thank goodness you've arrived! I don't know what's going on—I really don't . . . I mean—where am I going to put everything? And what about insurance . . .?'

Leonie looked at her mother in astonishment.

'What's the matter?' she asked, hanging up Jade's coat as the small girl ran off into the sitting-room.

'It was all those men, you see.' The older woman sighed and brushed a tired hand through her grey hair. 'You've simply no idea—I mean, the doorbell hasn't stopped ringing all morning! It was: "Sign here" and "Sign there", till I thought I'd go mad.'

'Mother, for heaven's sake, calm down! I haven't a clue what you're talking about and—*Jade . . .!*' Leonie gasped as her daughter came back into the hall. 'What *do* you think you're wearing?'

'There—you see!' Mrs Elliot exclaimed as she and her daughter stared at the small girl pirouetting in front of them. What appeared to be a diamond tiara was set on her dark head, while two long, glittering strands of a diamond necklace dangled down over her short blue dress.

'Mummy—Mummy! Do look at me. Don't I look stu-pen-dous?' Jade laughed happily as the tiara slipped sideways to hang drunkenly down over her ear.

'Take it off, at once,' Leonie commanded, before turning to her mother in bewilderment. 'They can't possibly be . . .? I mean—they aren't *real* diamonds, are they?'

'The man from the jewellers assured me that they were. But that's not all—not by a long chalk!' Mrs Elliot said. Catching hold of Jade, and ignoring the little girl's protests, she firmly removed the sparkling jewellery. 'The sitting-room has become nothing more nor less than an Aladdin's Cave! Come and see for yourself.'

'Oh, my G-God!' Leonie stuttered, as with incredulous eyes she viewed the overflowing boxes piled high on every table and chair. 'Where did all this stuff come from?'

'Well, all the jewellery comes from Aspreys,' Mrs Elliot waved a distracted hand towards a mound of black leather cases. 'They are mostly sapphires and diamonds, I think, although maybe there was an emerald necklace as well.' She shook her head bemusedly and walked over to the drinks cabinet. 'God knows, I don't usually drink in the middle of the day, but I suddenly find myself in dire need of some alcohol!'

'But . . . but who . . .?'

'Well, dear, I really think it must be Badyr, don't you? I mean—who else do you know with enough money to buy all these things? Her mother sighed heavily and took a large sip from her glass. 'Now, what else? Oh, yes,' she added as Jade excitedly delved into a large box and pulled out a dark brown fur coat. 'When the man from the shop told me how much that sable coat was worth, I nearly had hysterics! And as for all those parcels of pure silk and satin underwear from The White House, they must have cost a fortune. Of course, it's wonderfully generous of Badyr,' she added quickly, 'but where on earth are we going to put everything? You should see the dining-room—it's full to the brim with what must be at least ten years' supply of cosmetics! Do you think you could possibly have a word with him and . . . er . . . explain that we haven't much room?'

'Damn right, I will—*the rat!*' Leonie snapped furiously, before remembering that Jade was in the room. Hastily clamping her lips tightly together, she removed the fur coat from her daughter and took Jade out to the kitchen to give the little girl her midday meal. When she rejoined her mother some time later, she found her sitting slumped in an armchair.

'You really must be careful not to . . .'

'I know, Mother,' Leonie sighed. 'I shouldn't have said what I did in front of Jade, but I was just so mad at Badyr! He knows—only too well—that the temperature in Dhoman has got to be at least a hundred degrees in the shade, and I'll need a fur coat like . . . like a hole in the head! As for chucking his money around like an oriental millionaire—those diamonds alone must have cost enough to feed everyone in his beastly, fly-blown country for at least a month. What a swine the man is!'

'Leonie! How can you say that when Badyr's been so ... so ...'

'Diabolically sure of himself?' Leonie gave a shrill, hysterical laugh. 'You can't possibly imagine that Badyr went out and bought all these things this morning? There's no way he could have completed the purchases *and* had everything delivered by now. In fact—I haven't a shred of doubt that the bloody man had already ordered everything *before* he saw me last night. He knew damn well that his blackmail couldn't fail—and all these things,' she added, glaring about the room as she lifted the telephone receiver. 'They're nothing but sugar icing on the bars of my prison cell!'

Her call to his suite at Claridges was answered by Sheikh Samir. 'Would you kindly tell my husband *not* to send me items for which I have no use!' she snapped. 'It's a quite ridiculous waste of his time and money, and ...'

'Ah, Leonie.' Badyr's rich, dark voice came on the line, interrupting her carefully prepared speech. 'I wish to talk to you about seeing my daughter.'

'There's nothing to stop you seeing her whenever you wish, and it's certainly a better use of your time than buying up the whole of Bond Street!' she grated angrily.

Infuriatingly, he merely gave a low, mocking laugh as he ignored her caustic remark. 'Since you clearly have no objection, I will call and see Jade tomorrow, at three o'clock. We will take her to Regent's Park Zoo, yes?'

'No.' Leonie knew that she was reacting childishly, but why should she have to keep jumping through his hoops? 'It will ... um ... be much too cold at this time of year,' she improvised quickly, desperately trying to think of an alternative venue.

'Jade is unwell?'

'No, of course not—she's in perfectly good health!'
she retorted quickly.

'Then you will only need to wrap her up warmly,
hmm? As for yourself, you now have a fur coat, my
dear Leonie. I therefore suggest that you wear it!' His
sardonic laugh was cut short as he put down the
phone before she could think of a suitably crushing
reply.

Both Leonie and her mother spent some time that
evening explaining to Jade that her father was in
England, and would be coming to see her tomorrow.
The little girl was so excited at the prospect that it
proved a difficult task to persuade her to go to bed, and
a long time before she at last fell asleep.

Leonie discovered that she also found sleep elusive,
and subsequently she overslept the next morning.
Thereafter, the day seemed to be one in which she never
quite managed to catch up with the work awaiting her
at the office and, as always happened when she needed
to get away early, the phone never stopped ringing. As
a consequence she was late arriving home, noting with
dismay the large chauffeur-driven limousine that was
parked outside the house.

She felt sick with apprehension, but was determined
not to show it as she took a deep breath and entered the
sitting-room. She found Jade sitting happily perched on
Badyr's knee, busily engaged in placing his black patch
over her own small eye.

'How do I look, Mummy?' she demanded, before
jumping up and running over to stand on a stool,
regarding herself critically in a mirror for several
moments. 'I don't think I look as nice as Daddy,' she
added thoughtfully, running back to climb up on to her
father's lap.

Leonie couldn't say anything for a moment. There
seemed to be a large lump in her throat, her body
trembling with shock at the sight of the two dark heads
so close together. Why had she never realised just what

a strong resemblance there was between father and child?

Badyr smiled lazily down at Jade, idly playing with a lock of her black, shoulder-length hair. 'She is very much my daughter, hmm?' he murmured softly, accurately reading Leonie's mind.

Who else's daughter should she be? Leonie wanted to scream, biting her lip with frustration as she realised that to relieve her feelings by snapping at Badyr would only upset Jade. The little girl was bouncing with excitement as she wound her arms about Badyr's neck.

'It's so nice to have a real daddy, at last!' she sighed happily. 'Are we really going to Ar-ab-ia? Mummy's pretty, isn't she? She was very cross about the fur coat and the diamonds. In fact . . .' Jade grinned at her mother, '. . . I heard her say some *very* naughty words to Grandma—I really did! Are you going to give me some diamonds too? I do hope so, 'cos you see, Jill— she's my best friend at school, although I hate her really—well, she has a pink pearl necklace. But, if I had some of those stu-pen-dous diamonds, then she would be terribly cross . . . I'd like that!'

Leonie could barely manage to repress a malicious grin as she watched her husband mentally reeling under the rapid fire of Jade's artless conversation. 'Very much your daughter, I think you said!' she murmured, before telling the little girl to go and get her coat.

'Is she always quite so . . . er . . . talkative?' he enquired with a broad grin.

'Oh, no, not at all!' Leonie deliberately made her voice saccharin-sweet. 'Jade's still feeling a little shy, of course, but when she knows you better, I can promise you that she'll be *far* more forthcoming!'

'Then I can see that life will certainly not be boring!' His broad shoulders shook with laughter as Jade danced back into the room.

'Hurry up, Daddy. I want to see the camels and the snakes and . . .'

'I am quite ready, little one. We are merely waiting for your mother to put on her fur coat, are we not? The one about which I understand she was so ... er ... cross, hmm?'

It would have given Leonie great pleasure to have been able to slap the mocking smile off his handsome face. As it was, there was nothing she could do but go and put the damn thing on! And as much as she hated to admit it, even to herself, she couldn't help but relish the warmth and feel of the luxurious fur as they left the car to enter the zoo.

Preoccupied in keeping an eye on Jade as she scampered off towards one of the cages, Leonie looked up startled to see Badyr's tall figure standing in front of her.

'You must be careful not to catch cold,' he said, his voice heavy with irony as he reached forward, lifting the shawl collar of her coat about her ears. 'Incidentally, if I should decide to give my wife some jewellery, or dress her as befits her station in life, I do not expect her to argue with me. Do I make myself clear?' he murmured with soft menace.

'Please let me go!' she demanded, trying in vain to move her head away from the firm grasp of his hands beneath the fur collar, the words coming from her throat in a tremulous, hoarse whisper and not the imperious command that she intended. As he continued to stare searchingly down into her blue eyes, she desperately tried to steel herself against the dynamic masculinity exuded by the man standing so close to her quivering figure. But there seemed nothing she could do to prevent a deep flush from staining her cheeks, or her breathing from becoming ragged and uneven.

He gave her a slow, sensual smile. 'How very, very remiss of me—I have not yet thanked you for giving me such a lovely daughter, and for bestowing on her such a beautiful name. Can it be that you still have my ring, Leonie . . .?'

'I ... er ...' she faltered, her sapphire blue eyes unable to meet his dark gaze. She was only too well aware of the large jade signet ring, carefully wrapped in tissue paper and buried at the bottom of her small jewel-box. On leaving Dhoman she had gladly left behind all the jewellery she had been given by Badyr, retaining only his signet ring which he had put on her finger a day before their wedding; the purchase of an engagement ring having been forgotten in the hasty preparations for their marriage.

'No matter,' he murmured, his voice breaking into her confusion and rescuing her from having to reply. 'If Jade grows up to be as beautiful as her mother, I shall indeed be happy.'

The husky note in his voice should have warned her, but Leonie was too concerned with striving to control her own wayward emotions to react in time. Almost before she knew what was happening, she found herself clasped tightly in his arms and responding without thought to the seduction of the firm lips possessing her own. An ever-swelling tide of excitement raced through her body, her senses reeling swiftly out of control, and it was only Jade's impatient pull on the fur coat which brought her back to reality.

'Do come and see the elephants, Daddy—they're gi-nor-mous! What are you kissing Mummy for? I'm awfully hungry, so can we go and have an ice-cream, please?' Jade clasped Badyr's hand as he released Leonie's trembling figure, tugging him off towards a kiosk.

Damn, damn, damn! Leonie cursed silently as she turned away to gaze blindly at a pair of long-necked, languid giraffes. What on earth had come over her? It was no good trying to pretend, even to herself, that she hadn't been responding to his kiss—because she most certainly had. And in the middle of the zoo, for heaven's sake! What was more: that stupid, emotional gesture of naming her daughter after Badyr's ring—

something which had once meant so much to her—
seemed to be giving him *quite* the wrong ideas! A deep
tide of crimson flooded over her face as she recognised
the ache in her treacherous body, the reason why her
legs felt like jelly and her hands were shaking so badly.
She had been so sure, so positive after all these years,
that Badyr's strong physical presence would no longer
have the power to disturb her. A heavy lump of shame
and depression gripped her stomach as she realised just
how wrong her assumptions had been.

She somehow managed to stagger through the
remainder of their visit to the zoo, careful to avoid
meeting the mocking, sardonic gleam in Badyr's dark
eyes. The only morsel of comfort, despite any worries
Leonie might have had, was that Jade had enthusiastically taken to her father, who seemed to be equally
enslaved by his daughter.

'Yes, I promise that I will see you tomorrow, little
one,' he assured the child as they arrived back at the
house. 'Maybe you would like to come and have tea
with me in my hotel?'

'Oh, yes, please!' Jade breathed ecstatically, leaping
out of the vehicle and dashing into the house to tell her
grandmother all about her wonderful day.

'I'm afraid that my mother will have to accompany
Jade tomorrow,' Leonie muttered nervously as she
prepared to get out of the car. 'I'm very busy at work at
the moment, clearing my desk and . . .'

'Relax, Leonie!' Badyr murmured, catching hold of
her elbow and halting her hurried exit. 'Once we have
returned to Dhoman, we will have all the time in the
world to be alone together, hmm?'

'No!' she gasped. 'That's not what I meant at all. I
really am busy, and . . .'

'I know what you meant,' he interrupted smoothly.
'But I also meant what I said to you the other night.
For the moment, and until such time as we return to my
country, I will permit you to enjoy your single bed.

However, let there be no doubt in your mind,' he warned her with cool, silky menace. 'When you return to Dhoman, it will be as my wife—in every sense of the word!'

'Who do you think you are—God's gift to women?' she demanded breathlessly, her blue eyes flashing with rage. 'I ... I've told you, quite clearly, that I can't possibly ... that I won't ever ...'

Badyr gave a low bark of dry, sardonic laughter. 'Oh, yes, my dear Leonie, you will find that you can, and indeed you will!'

Leonie was still seething, burning with indignation at her invidious position, when she went to spend the evening with Sally a week later. They had supper in her friend's flat, giggling like young girls as they passed on to each other some of the latest gossip about old school friends.

'It's been such fun,' Leonie sighed. 'Just to be able to forget about everything for a few hours has been marvellous.'

'Does your husband really expect ...?' Sally paused. 'I mean, does he really imagine that you can both just resume your relationship together, after all these years, as if nothing had happened?' she queried, having listened earlier in the evening to Leonie's account of Badyr's sudden reappearance in her life.

'I know—the whole idea is crazy, isn't it? We've both changed so much during the last five years. Badyr is now a much harder, tougher character than the man I married, while I ...' She shrugged. 'Well, the past five years haven't exactly been a piece of cake, but I have managed to hold down a good job and support myself and Jade. Let's face it,' her voice hardened with exasperation, 'there's no way I bear any resemblance to the young, starry-eyed girl he married years ago. And how he expects me to fall on his neck with a grateful sigh at being taken back to that hateful country, is quite beyond me! Are all men so conceited, I wonder?'

'Every single one of them that I've ever met!' Sally grinned. 'Still, being showered by diamonds and a fabulous fur coat can't be all bad?'

'That was just the beginning!' Leonie groaned. 'The damned man must have spent I don't know how much money—practically buying up London, for heaven's sake! It seems as though the doorbell has never stopped ringing with the delivery of one huge parcel after another; honestly, Sally, it's completely unbelievable—both Mother and I are becoming demented! The house is overflowing with boxes and boxes: hundreds of pairs of shoes from Rayne, Gucci and Charles Jourdan ... ditto handbags; sapphire and diamond jewellery like you've never seen before in your life; crates of heavily monogrammed linen sheets, pillowcases and towels; huge flagons of my favourite scent...' She sighed heavily. 'The list is *endless ...!*'

Sally gaped in astonishment. 'It all sounds amazing!'

'Believe me—I can think of other words to describe the state we're in!' Leonie said with a grim laugh. 'My mother is reduced to taking tranquillisers by the handful—just to get herself through the day! And we both spend most of the night lying wide awake, expecting to be burgled any moment! Don't you dare laugh...' she added as her friend collapsed with giggles.

'I can't help it!' Sally gasped. 'How on earth are you going to pack and transport all those things to Dhoman?'

'Oh, my dear husband has solved that little problem,' Leonie ground out through clenched teeth. 'This morning's collection of goodies contained, among other items, monogrammed leather cases and trunks from Lowe of Bond Street—Jade even has her own set of luggage, but she's not particularly interested, of course. She's far keener on two brand-new saddles and bridles, which were despatched all the way from a shop in Newmarket. I imagine that they are for a pony, but since she hasn't got one and can't ride yet—your guess is as good as mine!'

'How does Jade feel about her father?' her friend asked, wiping the tears of laughter from her eyes.

'Well, obviously she thinks he's the best thing since sliced bread!' Leonie shrugged. 'Actually, to be fair, she'd adore him even if he hadn't a bean and just swept streets for a living. They ... well, they're both very alike, very much in tune with each other.'

'And ... er ... apart from all his quite extraordinary largesse, how do you feel about Badyr, himself?' Sally asked quietly. 'Are you ... well, do you still find him attractive?'

'Are you kidding?' Leonie retorted quickly. 'Absolutely, one hundred per cent not! I really hate the man—anything I once felt for him has long since disappeared. I mean ... how would you feel about a man who virtually abandoned you for five years?'

'I don't know,' Sally replied slowly, staring at the hectic flush on her friend's cheeks. She didn't believe that Leonie was being entirely honest with herself, but there seemed little point in pressing the point and she turned the conversation into safer channels.

However, as she stood chatting to Leonie at Mrs Elliot's wedding reception some five days later, Sally could hardly tear her eyes away from the tall dark figure of Badyr. She had noticed him in the church earlier that morning, and now he was standing across the room talking to Leonie's cousin, Janet, who was gazing up at him with dazed eyes.

'Is that really your husband? I didn't know he was going to be here,' she whispered.

'Neither did I!' Leonie hissed out of the corner of her mouth, glaring at the back of his broad shoulders. 'The damned man simply turned up without any warning. He's supposed to be taking Jade and me away after this reception, so I imagine that he's just making sure we don't have a chance to disappear—the swine!'

'But, Leonie, he's ... he's *stunning*! And with that black patch and scar, *well ...*'

'Got a "thing" for pirates have you?' Leonie sniffed dismissively.

'Oh, come on! You, my girl, are protesting far too much,' Sally murmured. 'He's devastatingly attractive, and well you know it! So, I may add, does every other woman at this reception. Look at them—they're all staring at him with glazed eyes. Honestly, Leonie, I've never seen so many bosoms heaving and panting with sheer lust ...!'

'You always were a nasty, vulgar girl at school, and I can see you haven't changed one little bit!' Leonie sternly told her friend, who merely grinned as Jade came running up to join them.

'Daddy says that we've got to go soon,' she announced excitedly. 'And we don't have to go home and get changed. Daddy says that I look so pretty in my dress that I can wear it on the aeroplane! Don't I look nice, Aunt Sally?'

'You look lovely,' Sally assured her, admiring the flounces of cream satin and lace. 'It's a simply wonderful dress, Leonie. Wherever did you buy it?'

'Me? You must be joking? Little madam, here, took her father shopping in Harrods—where else?—and came home with that small item, among many others!' She smiled wryly down at her daughter. 'Of course, Jade is just a *little* disappointed that she hasn't got a diamond tiara of her own to go with it—but she tells me she's working on it!'

The sound of Sally's laughter was so infectious that despite her general misery, Leonie found herself reluctantly joining in. Until the smile was wiped off her face as she felt a strong hand firmly grasp her arm.

'I think, my dear Leonie, that it is time you said your farewells,' Badyr murmured quietly, his dark gaze sweeping with appreciation over her slim figure in a finely pleated dress of pearl grey silk shantung and the small, veiled hat decorated with grey and pink roses.

'But I can't possibly go before Mother and Clifford leave for their honeymoon. And ... and I've got to change, and ...'

'I have arranged matters with your mother and her new husband. There is also no need to change your clothes, since we shall, of course, be driven straight to my aeroplane,' he said firmly.

'But ...'

'I will allow you five minutes. However, if you are not back by my side in that time,' he added blandly, 'you may be very sure that I will have you forcibly removed from this room.'

She glared angrily up at the man surveying her flushed cheeks and furious eyes with cynical detachment. Tense and trembling with nervous tension, she tried to muster the courage to defy him. But she couldn't. She knew—only too well—that she had no choice but to obey his commands.

Tightly compressing her lips to stop herself from giving vent to her rage and frustration, Leonie turned and walked across the room. Moving like an automaton, she calmly kissed her mother and new stepfather, and said goodbye to all her friends and relatives. It was as if she had become totally numb, aware of nothing but the sickening knowledge which lay heavy as lead in her stomach.

With Jade as his hostage for her good behaviour, Badyr would be able to enforce any and all of his demands for the foreseeable future ... and there wasn't going to be a damn thing she could do about it!

CHAPTER FIVE

LEONIE lay soaking in the deep, sunken marble bath, gazing at her opulent surroundings with bemusement. After the last two weeks of wretched misery, forcing herself to face up to and accept the inevitability of her return to the dreaded Harem, it seemed impossible to believe that she would be living in this luxurious new palace, whose large airy rooms seemed another world away from the dark, dank old fortress that she remembered so well. This place was ... well, it was magnificent! She had been amazed by the size of Jade's suite, let alone the beautifully decorated, elegant rooms allocated to her own use.

A tired frown creased her brow as she stared up at the pink marble ceiling. Exhausted by the long flight and anxious to settle Jade down to sleep, she hadn't really had the time, or the opportunity, to question Badyr on the exact sleeping arrangements here in the new palace. Was this wing of the building a modern version of the old Harem, where Sultan Raschid had possessed his own private suite, and visited his two wives in strict nightly rotation as laid down in the Koran—the Moslem bible? She fervently hoped that Badyr had separate quarters, otherwise it was going to be extremely difficult, if not impossible, for her to avoid him.

The imperative need to keep well away from her husband's orbit had been only too clearly demonstrated during the long, seven-hour flight from London. Silent and numb with misery as she boarded Badyr's privately-owned Boeing 727, she was briefly introduced to the crew and a sandy-haired, freckle-faced girl called Elizabeth Jackson, who was apparently to be Jade's new governess. Leonie's resentment at her husband's high-handed behaviour in not consulting her about the appointment was further exacerbated by the fact that Badyr gave her no opportunity to object to his decision. Shortly after take-off, and blandly ignoring her rebellious expression, he ordered a young Arab stewardess to escort his wife to one of the small private bedrooms on the aircraft.

'I wish you to rest, and therefore Miss Jackson will be looking after Jade during the flight,' Badyr said, calmly disregarding her protest at being removed from her child.

'But I'm not at all tired, and ...'

'I am not prepared to discuss the matter. Kindly do as you are told,' he added coldly, before turning away to have a word with Sheikh Samir.

Embarrassingly, aware of the hovering stewardess, Leonie almost screamed with frustration. It was clear that short of having a full-scale row, the only result of which would be to seriously disturb Jade, she had no alternative but to obey Badyr's command. Smouldering with fury, she allowed herself to be conducted to her cabin, and it was of little comfort to realise that the damned man had been right—that she had indeed been tired and nervously exhausted—when she found herself being shaken awake some hours later. Leonie felt confused for a moment and then recognised the continuous hum of the engines and the face of the stewardess, who was placing a cup of tea on the small table bolted to the floor beside her bed.

'The Sultan has asked me to say that we shall be landing at Dhoman in just over two hours, Majesty. Is there anything you require—anything I can do for you?'

Leonie struggled to sit up, brushing a weary hand through her long, curly hair as the young stewardess plumped up the pillows behind her back.

'I ... I'm fine, thank you. But, my daughter ...?'

'The Princess is still fast asleep, although I can wake her if you wish.'

'No, I'd prefer her to rest as long as possible. Thank you for the tea,' Leonie smiled at the girl. 'It's very welcome.'

'A pleasure, Majesty,' the stewardess murmured as she left the room.

Leonie reached over for the cup and saucer, sighing heavily as she stared down at the pale brown liquid. All this 'Majesty' and 'Princess' business—she'd have to have a word with Badyr about it as soon as possible. Otherwise Jade, who was a very ordinary little girl, was likely to become a nasty spoilt brat—especially if Badyr continued to give his daughter everything her heart desired. While as for herself? Never in a million years could she become used to being addressed as a queen— although the thought of being called 'Sultana' was even worse!

Getting out of bed and walking through into the small adjacent bathroom, she gazed glumly at her reflection in the mirror. Well, 'a dried-up grape' wasn't a bad description of how she looked at the moment, she told herself, viewing the thick cloud of uncombed hair and the shadows beneath her blue eyes. In fact, she looked simply dreadful! Although—God knows—the strain and nervous tension of the last two weeks would have aged anyone.

However, her spirits began to lift as she discovered that the small bathroom contained a shower. Standing under the fine needle-spray of warm water, Leonie couldn't help worrying about her imminent arrival at Dhoman. Where on earth did Badyr think she was going to wear all those clothes and jewels he had bought in London? Locked away in the Harem, she wasn't going to see anyone—or be seen, for that matter. At the thought of the long years of isolation ahead of her, she had to grit her teeth to prevent the weak tears from sliding down her cheeks. All this luxury was a hollow comfort and meant nothing without personal liberty. And as for the man who was going to lock her up and then throw away the key . . . How could Badyr possibly expect her to feel anything for him, other than fear and animosity?

However, by the time she had made up her face and slipped into a blue silk dress, she felt slightly calmer. There was absolutely no point in giving way to self-pity, she told herself firmly. Why give Badyr the satisfaction of knowing just how miserable she was? After all, this time she knew what she would be facing, and had prepared for it. She managed to grin shakily at herself in the mirror, remembering the grunts and groans of the men at Heathrow as they had loaded up one of her trunks into the aircraft. Only she knew that it was full to the brim with books of every description: from a complete set of the *Encyclopaedia Britannica*, and volumes of self-tuition in over twelve languages—together with all the necessary dictionaries—down to as many paperback novels as she had been able to lay her hands on.

She had calculated that she would have to stay in Dhoman for at least the next eleven years, by which time Jade would be sixteen, grown up and well able to live her own life. Then, there would be nothing Badyr could do to prevent his wife from escaping back to the West, no blackmail that he could exert to keep her in a country that she so detested. And when that longed-for day arrived: she might well be an old hag of thirty-six—but at least, Leonie grimly promised herself, she was going to be a well-educated old hag!

A knock at the door interrupted her thoughts, the stewardess quietly announcing that there was a cold meal awaiting her in the forward saloon, and that Jade was still fast asleep.

Glancing quickly at her watch, Leonie saw that there was well over an hour to go before they landed.

Deciding to let Jade rest as long as possible, she took a deep breath and left the bedroom.

Going into the main part of the aircraft, she saw that it was divided into two, with Badyr, Sheikh Samir and two other men talking quietly together in an office, which was separated from the lounge area by sliding glass walls. Nervously trying to ignore the quick turn of Badyr's head and his searching glance, she followed the stewardess over to the high-backed, comfortable plush chairs surrounding a round dining-table. It was only as she sat down that she realised she wasn't alone.

'It's a long journey, isn't it?'

'Yes ... yes it is,' Leonie answered, looking at the strange girl's friendly, freckled face and realising that she must be Elizabeth Jackson, Jade's new governess.

'I ... er ... I believe that you are coming to Dhoman to teach my daughter,' she said as cold meat and salads were placed on the table. 'Has my husband told you anything about the country?'

'Not a great deal,' the girl smiled. 'However, Jade seems to be a very intelligent little girl, and I'm looking forward both to teaching her, and my first visit to the Middle East.'

'I don't want to put you off before you've even started your job, Miss Jackson,' Leonie said wryly as she passed the salad bowl. 'But it seems only fair to warn you that if I had to think of a word to describe your future surroundings, possibly "primitive" would best fit the bill.'

The girl laughed. 'Well, Mrs ... er ... Your Majesty ...'

'Oh, please,' she quickly interjected. 'My name is Leonie, and I'll call you Elizabeth, if I may, okay?'

'Fair enough—just as long as the Sultan doesn't object to such *lèse-majesté*?'

Leonie found herself grinning with wry amusement at the girl's apt pun, and began to feel considerably more cheerful at the thought of not being entirely on her own in Dhoman. 'Have you always been a governess?' she asked, staring down at her plate with distaste. She didn't feel able to face any food, however beautifully prepared.

'Well, I spent some years teaching in various primary schools,' Elizabeth said. 'And then, two years ago, I took a job as private tutor to the young children of the Kuwaiti Ambassador—which is how I came to be recommended to your husband. I really am a good teacher, even if it's immodest for me to say so!' She smiled reassuringly at the beautiful woman sitting oppposite, who seemed strangely tense and nervous.

'However, I've now reached the age of thirty, and looking back I couldn't see that I'd done anything very exciting with my life. So, I decided that I'd like a challenge, a bit of adventure before I finally became a crabby old maid. Which is why,' she concluded, 'I jumped at the chance of deepest Arabia! I honestly don't care how rough or primitive it turns out to be— and I promise you that I'll make sure your daughter has the best education I can give her. Okay?'

'Okay.' Leonie's lips curved into a brief smile. She privately thought that the new governess was selling herself short. She wasn't a beauty, of course, but with an infectious smile and twinkling brown eyes, she presented a warm, attractive personality.

A slight popping in her ears indicated that the plane was beginning to lose height, and it wouldn't be too long before they landed. She rose from the table to go and see to Jade. The little girl had just woken up, still very sleepy and lethargic as she allowed herself to be changed into a thin cotton dress, before Leonie handed her over to Elizabeth while she went to gather her own things together.

Busily engaged in packing her case, Leonie nearly jumped out of her skin as the bathroom door opened and Badyr entered the room.

'What are you doing in here?' she gasped, noting that

he had discarded his Savile Row suit, and was now clothed in his national dress. The sight of his tall figure in the long white robes brought back such poignant, disturbing memories, that her trembling figure swayed and would have fallen if Badyr hadn't moved swiftly forward to put an arm about her waist.

'Husbands and wives normally share the same room,' he drawled softly as his grip tightened. 'Or did you expect me to change my clothes in the main cabin, hmm?'

'No ... I ...' Leonie swallowed nervously. The elusive aromatic scent of his cologne and the close proximity of his hard, masculine form seemed to be having a disastrous effect on her nervous system, and making her shockingly aware of the emotional response of her own body. What was happening to her? How could she possibly feel like this about someone from whom she had been parted for so long? A man who had threatened to abduct her child, and who was forcing her to return to a country she hated? It simply didn't make any kind of sense—none at all. Turning her head away, she closed her eyes as she fought to control the deep flush staining her cheeks, gasping as she felt him pluck the combs from her hair.

'What do you think you're doing?' she protested nervously as the thick, reddish-gold curls fell about her shoulders.

'Merely admiring your crowning glory,' he murmured, running his hand through her heavy mass of hair. 'And, since we have a bed at our disposal—it would seem a shame not to use it, hmm?' His soft, mocking laugh echoed ominously around the small room. Trying to twist away, she realised that she was hopelessly trapped, his fingers tightening in her hair and holding her head firmly imprisoned beneath him.

Her instinctive denial was smothered as his warm mouth possessed hers, moving softly and sensuously over her lips and evoking a trembling response almost impossible to resist. Every nerve-end in her body seemed to be tingling with excitement, a deep knot of tremulous desire flaring into pulsating life as her arms slid up about his neck and her lips parted involuntarily under the delicate pressure, allowing him to slowly and erotically savour the soft moistness within.

Badyr's husky murmur of satisfaction at her action did nothing to encourage her resistance. She seemed powerless to prevent her body becoming soft and pliant as he moulded it to his own, his hands moving down over her back to span her slim waist before reaching her hips. It was only when he relaxed his grip to lower her down on to the bed that sanity returned. It seemed to require an almost super-human effort to break away from the intoxication of his kiss and the seductive caress of the hands now savouring the rounded warmth of her breasts, but she eventually managed to pull her shattered mind and body together.

'No!' she gasped, jerking back her head and striving to push him away. Panting breathlessly, her dazed eyes noted his sardonic grin as he let her go and rose to his feet.

'Poor Leonie—you look somewhat disturbed!' he said softly, gazing down at her trembling figure. 'It would seem that your claim of amnesia was merely a temporary affliction!' His low, cynical laugh was hateful, adding fuel to the flames of her self-disgust as she quickly rose from the bed on legs which felt as if they were made of cotton wool.

'I don't know what you're talking about,' she muttered, inwardly cursing the betraying, husky note in her voice. Moving jerkily over to a mirror, she attempted to scoop her hair back up on top of her head, the coiled, nervous tension in her shaking hands making the task far more difficult than usual.

'You lie!' Badyr said curtly. 'Your body is crying out for my possession—just as much as mine demands release. It is pointless to deny it.'

She gave a shrill, incredulous laugh. 'You can't seriously imagine that you're the only man who ... who ...'

'Can raise you to the height of ecstasy, and far beyond?' he queried, moving slowly towards her trembling figure. 'We both know it is so, and the sooner you acknowledge the fact, the better it will be for both of us.'

'You ... you arrogant swine! I'll never do that— *never*!'

'Do not try my patience too far, Leonie.' His soft drawl held a warning that was impossible to ignore. Viewing in the mirror his tight lips and the stern cast of his countenance, she felt a frisson of fear shiver down her spine.

'We shall be landing in Dhoman shortly. I hope that you will not make the mistake of ever forgetting that I am now absolute ruler of my country,' he added, his voice heavy with menace. 'There is no route open to you, other than to obey my commands.' He paused for a moment. 'Unless, of course, you wish to lose your daughter.'

'You ... you *blackmailer*! You're every bit as evil as your old father!' she hissed through clenched teeth, shaking and trembling with the effort to control herself as she stalked over to the door. 'He was a fool to have locked you up in prison. If he hadn't been so crazy, he'd have known that he should have polished you off while he had the chance, and ... and made me a thoroughly merry widow!'

She might have felt happier if her Parthian shot as she slammed the door of the small cabin hadn't been followed by his low rumble of sardonic laughter, the sound echoing in her ears as she made her way into the main lounge area.

Later, as she adjusted the straps about Jade's sleepy figure, Leonie cursed her own folly. She was bitterly ashamed at her pitiful lack of resistance, her pathetic, emotional weakness as far as Badyr was concerned. She had taken great care to avoid all meetings with him—ever since that disastrous episode at the zoo—*and how right she'd been!* She didn't know how she was going to evade any further contact with him, but the Harem quarters in that grim old fort were full of deserted corridors and long-forgotten rooms. Maybe, if she kept her wits about her, she could ensure that she escaped his presence?

Carrying Jade down the steps of the aeroplane, Leonie felt as if she was walking into a hot Turkish bath. A wall of heat came up to meet her, the dark night air carrying an unforgettable smell of the lingering effects of burning sun on sand, tarmac and machines, mingled with the evocative aroma of frankincense and other aromatic spices so peculiar to Dhoman.

It was all so extraordinarily familiar, that she half expected to see one of the late Sultan Raschid's old cars come lurching up to the aircraft. Instead of which, a fleet of black limousines moved smoothly forward and together with Elizabeth and Jade, Leonie was led towards a black Rolls-Royce with dark-tinted windows.

'It's all very luxurious, isn't it?' Elizabeth said, looking about the plush interior of the car as it slowly moved away across the tarmac.

'Purdah,' Leonie muttered, in answer to the other girl's puzzled glance at the windows. 'It is the custom in Arabia to make sure that the male sex aren't tempted to run amok with unbridled lust, and so women are hidden from their gaze at all times—hence the dark windows. I suspect that my husband will have failed to mention an important facet of your future life,' she added. 'Namely, that you will be living in a Harem—the women's quarters of the palace—and from which you will seldom, if ever, be released.' She sighed and shrugged her shoulders. 'However—welcome to Dhoman, Miss Jackson!'

Silence fell in the car, Elizabeth digesting the

information she had just been given, while Leonie
cuddled the sleeping form of her daughter and stared
blindly out of the window. It was still night, and there
was little to be seen, although she was surprised to note
that they seemed to be travelling along a wide highway,
brilliantly lit by modern sodium lamps; very different
from the conditions under the old Sultan's regime.

The journey seemed to take a surprisingly long time,
but at last the car slowed down, the wheels crunching
over gravel before the vehicle came at last to a halt. The
door was jerked open, the lights dazzling their eyes as
the two women descended from the Rolls.

'*Wow!*' Elizabeth breathed.

Wow ... indeed! Leonie thought, looking about her
in utter confusion. Instead of the grim, grey exterior of
the old fort, her startled eyes swept over a long, white,
two-storied modern building. The tall windows, shaped
like Moorish arches, were ablaze with light which spilled
out on to the forecourt and illuminated the wide
expanse of green lawn. She was staring in awed
fascination at the elegant pools surrounding the
mansion, whose cascading fountains were lit from
below, when she saw Badyr walking slowly down the
wide steps towards her, the long white robes flowing
dramatically about his tall, elegant figure.

'Ah, you have arrived at last,' he murmured, his
lips twitching with amusement at the incomprehension
on her face as he led her up the stairs and into the
building.

'I don't understand,' she muttered. 'What ... I mean,
what's happened to the old palace?'

'It has been demolished,' Badyr said flatly. 'I decided
to build a new home well outside the old town, and this
is now my principal residence here in Muria. It is a
definite improvement on the old palace, wouldn't you
say, hmm?'

'I certainly would!' Leonie gasped, looking around at
the wide expanse of white marble flooring in the

entrance hall, the tall elegant columns which supported the high-domed ceiling way above her head. 'It's absolutely beautiful—and *definitely* an improvement on that ghastly old fort!'

They smiled broadly at each other, Leonie forgetting for a moment her mistrust of the man beside her in the shared memories of the ancient, grimly forbidding old castle. It wasn't until Jade gave a tired moan of protest that she had been recalled to the need to see to her daughter's comfort.

Now, lying here in the warm scented water, Leonie's head was still spinning as she tried to come to terms with her new environment. It was clear that Badyr hadn't, after all, been lying about providing her with a new home. Did that also mean that he would allow her more freedom of movement as he had promised? The brief feeling of optimism which swept through her tired body was sharply and abruptly terminated a moment later. She must be out of her mind! How could she have possibly forgotten the scene in the aeroplane and the other firm promise—the quite definite statement he had made in London . . .?

A knock at the door interrupted her distracted thoughts, the feverish flush, which had swept through her body at the recollection of Badyr's determination to exercise his 'husbandly rights', dying away as her old servant entered the room. She had been delighted to see Hussa again, a happiness fully reciprocated by the Arab woman, who had greeted her former mistress with tears of joy running down her cheeks.

'Ah, Majesty, all has been arranged. Your clothes have been put away in the cupboards and a small meal awaits you in the other room.' Hussa clicked her teeth as she came over and insisted on scrubbing Leonie's back. 'You must not stay in the bath too long. Your skin will become dry and wrinkled—and that will not please your husband, eh?' she cackled with laughter.

'This is a wonderful new palace,' Leonie said quickly,

anxious not to discuss her relationship with Badyr.
'Does my husband's mother live here too?'

'Oh, no. The Sultana Zenobia and Princess Maryam
have their own palace a few miles away, and Sultana
Fatima and her daughters have also been provided with
a home. His Majesty has been good to his two mothers,
yes? And so busy! The country has changed overnight,
it seems. Yes, we are indeed blessed with our Sultan.
Day and night he has laboured to make all well for his
people. You cannot imagine the miles of new roads
from town to town, the new hospitals and schools for
the children—it is indeed a wonder what he has
achieved in the last five years.'

'Not before time!' Leonie muttered tersely, and then
immediately felt contrite. It wasn't Badyr's fault that
the reforms so desperately needed by the Dhomani
people had taken so long to be put into effect. And if
what Hussa said was true, then it would be churlish of
her not to give her husband full credit for all his hard
work.

'Now His Majesty will at last be truly happy with the
return of his beloved wife, eh? And the little princess—
so pretty, so like her father!' Hussa gave a deep sigh as
she stood up. 'I prayed that you would not lose the
baby you carried, and that the child would be born well
and strong. Praise be to Allah for his mercy, and for
listening to my prayers. I was so worried when you left
us, so frightened. You remember how it was, eh?' The
old serving woman gave another heavy sigh, and with a
stern reminder to Leonie not to remain in the bath too
long, she smiled and left the room.

Leonie climbed out of the bath, drying herself with
hands that shook with tension. Oh, yes, she remembered
how it was—only too well! Was it any wonder that she
had been frantic at having to come back to this country,
so deeply unhappy at being forced to become involved
with Badyr once again?

Slipping into the nightgown and matching négligé

which Hussa had put out for her, Leonie tried to calm her ragged nerves. It was only because she was tired and exhausted after the long journey, on top of the strain of the last two weeks, that she was allowing herself to lose her sense of proportion. What she needed was a good sleep, she told herself firmly, ignoring the food set out in the large sitting-room as she made her way into the enormous bedroom. Too fatigued to examine her surroundings properly, she slid between the sheets and a moment later was fast asleep.

She awoke to find the sun flooding into the room through the arched windows, the gauze curtains billowing in a soft breeze from the open casements. She gazed sleepily at the soft pink walls and the rose-coloured silk curtains which surrounded the windows, and which also fell in elegant loops and swags from the decorated cornice above the enormous bed. A small sound interrupted her lazy inspection, and raising her head she saw Badyr standing in the doorway which led to the bathroom.

'Ah, I see you are awake at last,' he murmured, walking slowly towards her across the white marble floor. Leonie idly noticed that he must have recently had a shower, since his black hair was still damp and he was wearing nothing but a short towel about his waist.

A shaft of sunlight caught his tall lithe figure, illuminating the smooth, golden-tanned skin rippling over the muscles of his arms and broad shoulders, the light mat of dark hair covering his deep chest. The passage of time had done nothing to diminish his powerful masculine attraction, nor the shivering response that gripped her stomach as she blinked nervously up at her husband. It was only when he sat down on the bed beside her that the alarm bells began to ring in her brain, breaking through the sleep-drugged mists of her mind with loud, strident urgency.

'What time is it?' she muttered, desperately trying to pull herself together.

'It is now ten in the morning, sleepy-head,' he smiled, his hand moving forward to toy with one of the tendrils of her long curly hair.

'Oh, my goodness! What about Jade?' She struggled to sit up. 'I must go and see to her immediately, I . . .'

'Be calm, my beloved, there is no need to worry. She has had her breakfast, and is now having her first riding lesson under the competent supervision of my Uncle Feisal and Miss Jackson.'

Leonie's nerves had begun to tingle at the soft emphasis he had placed on the endearment, a tide of crimson sweeping over her face as the gleaming dark eyes roamed slowly over the semi-nudity of her thin silk nightgown.

'It's very late. Oh, dear, I . . . um . . . I don't know how I could have slept so long. I must . . . yes, I must get up and . . . and get dressed,' she babbled, inching away from his tall, dominant figure.

'No, I don't think so, not just at the moment,' he drawled with soft mockery, his eyes glinting with sardonic amusement. 'I have . . . er . . . other plans for the next hour or two!'

'N-no . . .!' she stammered, giving up all attempts to pretend that she didn't fully understand his intentions. 'Please, no, Badyr. You . . . you don't really want me— you know you don't! There must be thousands of other women who . . .'

'Do not insult me, or yourself, Leonie. I can assure you that I know *exactly* what I want!'

The amusement had died from his face. His penetrating gaze, hard and unwavering, sent shock waves spiralling down her spine as she recognised the ruthless determination in the chilly depths of his dark eyes.

'No! Please—*no* . . .!' she gasped, attempting to scramble away across the bed, her progress abruptly halted as Badyr caught hold of her wrist in an iron grip.

She tried to pull away, but she found herself drawn relentlessly back towards his bare chest, gasping as his fingers tightened to crush her fragile bones. A tortured moan broke from her lips, and completely losing her temper she sank her teeth into his hand. Badyr gave a grunt of pain and released her arm, but as she snatched it away, he reached for her again and caught his fingers in the neck of her gown. There was a thin screeching sound as the silk gave way beneath the force of his action and the garment split from top to bottom.

A long silence followed as Leonie threw back her long, wild flowing locks, staring down in numb horror at the display of her own nakedness. She was unaware of Badyr's eyes devouring her glowing beauty: the sheen of her pale skin gleaming like pure alabaster in the warm morning light and the sight of her breasts, full and ripe, rising erotically between the torn fragments of material.

With a deep, husky growl of impatience he tore the towel from about his waist, moving swiftly to strip and toss aside the remnants of her nightgown. The next moment she found herself sprawled on her back, Badyr's hard body pinning her firmly to the mattress as he stared grimly down into her dazed eyes.

'*Wallahi!* Very well, my red-haired vixen—we shall see how long you can defy me!' he breathed heavily. 'And just how soon it is before you are begging for satisfaction, hmm?'

'Never!' she cried defiantly, beating her hands against his broad shoulders and trying to twist away from beneath his heavy weight. With contemptuous ease, Badyr captured first one hand and then the other, holding them firmly above her head and calmly allowing her to exhaust her strength in the vain attempt to escape him.

'I am a *very* patient man, Leonie,' he drawled softly as she lay panting wearily, and bitterly aware from the hardening muscles in his thighs that 'her desperate struggles had only served to increase his own arousal.

'After all, I have waited for five years, and so a few more minutes are neither here nor there, hmm?'

'I . . . I hate you! It . . . it's nothing but rape!' she gasped, tears of anger and frustration welling up in her blue eyes.

His lips curved into a savage smile. 'No, you do not hate me, nor will I have need of force. On the contrary, my sweet, you will shortly be pleading for the merciful release that only my possession can assuage!'

Her howl of protest was smothered as his mouth descended to cover hers, the bruising, relentless pressure forcing her lips apart and allowing him to savour the inner sweetness in a devastating invasion of her shattered senses. She was scarcely aware of exactly when the pressure eased and his mouth softened, moving over her trembling lips with a sensual languor that ignited a fire deep in her loins.

Leonie desperately tried to ignore the warmth of his lips as he kissed her damp eyelids and willed herself, with all the remaining strength at her command, not to respond to the mouth that trailed slowly over her cheek to murmur soft words of endearment in her ear. But as he continued, his lips scorching a path down her neck and on across the soft swell of her breasts, there was nothing she could do to prevent a helpless moan of pleasure, her body shuddering with ecstasy as his tongue caressed her nipples; the rosy peaks hardening with passion beneath his erotic touch. His mouth left her breasts to brush delicate kisses across her stomach, her body aching and throbbing at the promise of release from its long starvation, tremors of shock quivering through her flesh beneath the explicit sensuality of his mouth and hands.

Her emotions finally reeling completely out of control, she was only aware of the driving need to surrender to the passionate desire racing through her veins, the dizzy spiralling excitement engendered by the masterly seduction of his touch. Possessed by an urgent desire that went far beyond anything she had ever experienced before, her body writhed and arched against him, powerless against the explosive, ever-increasing ache that overrode all thought and action.

'Badyr—Badyr...!' The caressing hands and mouth moving over her body paused for a moment as she moaned his name in a helpless refrain.

'Umm?'

'Badyr ... *please*...!' she gasped, tormented by overwhelming desire as she feverishly pressed her lips against his hot, burning skin.

'Do you want me, Leonie?' His thick, husky whisper seemed to fill her whole existence.

'Oh, God! I ... I ... *Oh* ... *Y-Yes*...!'

With a harsh laugh of triumph, he swept his hands down over the sweet mounds of her breasts and the warm, undulating curve of her thighs, before parting her legs and possessing her with a thrusting, pulsating urgency that banished all conscious thought as their wild, physical rapture reached its climax.

Afterwards, as she lay silently within his arms, the realisation of her wanton response to his sensual mastery filled her with bitter shame. Fully intending to be as frigid as ice, she had been betrayed by her weak body into a raging inferno of passion.

'You see?' Badyr murmured softly, his fingers surprisingly gentle as he smoothed back the hair from her damp brow. 'There was no need for the "rape" that you spoke of, hmm?'

His words only served to deepen her humiliation. 'I loathe you for what you've just done—only slightly more than I hate and loathe myself,' she grated bleakly, unable to prevent her lips from trembling as tears began to trickle down her cheeks. 'How ... how often will I have to be ... be *used* in this way?'

He rolled his hard body over to cover her soft flesh, capturing her face with his hands and forcing her to meet the darkening gleam in his eyes.

'Ah, my beloved, how I love the way you hate!' he taunted softly, his mouth descending to brush away the escaping teardrops, before moving hungrily down to cover her quivering lips.

Her strangled moan was stifled as his kiss deepened, storming her puny defences and sending waves of heat pulsating through her body.

'I want you,' Badyr murmured thickly against her mouth, his words merely underlying the throbbing urgency of his body. 'And I will take you wherever and whenever I please. As for you, my dear wife . . . you will cry out for *my* possession, yearning for the intimate sweet pleasure that only *I* can give!'

Whimpering with despair, she found herself drowning in a deep pool of passion, before the hard pressure of his thighs ignited a flame of desire that was swiftly fanned into a white heat. Raging uncontrollably, it scorched through her body until she cried out—as he had said she would—eagerly demanding and welcoming his shuddering thrust and the sweeping, shattering sensation that exploded the universe around them into fragments of light and power.

CHAPTER SIX

'SWEET dreams, darling.' Leonie leant over to kiss Jade good night.

'Can I ride my pony tomorrow, Mummy?'

Leonie laughed. 'Since you've been riding nearly every day for the last four weeks, I don't suppose tomorrow will be any different, do you?'

'Great-uncle Feisal says I'm very good. He says that I show a natural ap-ti-tude!' Jade beamed up at her mother. 'Did you know that he can ride a camel? Yes, he can, really! He's going to show Miss Jackson how to do it, but he says I must learn to ride my pony first. Great-uncle Feisal is awfully nice, isn't he? In fact,' she paused, before adding the highest accolade in her vocabulary. 'In fact, I think he's stu-pen-dous!'

Leonie smiled. 'Come on, chatterbox. It's time you went to sleep.'

'It certainly is!'

The deep, mocking voice from behind her shoulder made Leonie jump. Badyr moves as silently as a panther—and he's every bit as unpredictable as one of those dangerous animals, she reminded herself, casting a sideways glance through her eyelashes at his profile as he sat down on the other side of Jade's bed.

'Doesn't Mummy look pretty?' Jade said, sitting up and winding her thin arms tightly about her father's neck. 'Are you going out tonight? I do wish I could come too.'

'You are much too young, little one!' Badyr laughed as he kissed her cheek and settled her back on the pillows. 'But yes, I agree that your mother is looking very pretty, and grows more lovely with each passing day.'

'Your father is apt to apply flattery with a shovel!'
Leonie said lightly, rising to her feet and blowing Jade a
good night kiss as she left the room. Walking back
down the corridor, a glance at her watch revealed that
there was no need for her to hurry. She had well over
an hour to get ready.

Entering her suite of rooms, Leonie wandered over to
the arched windows, sighing with pleasure as she gazed
down at the wide expanse of green lawn surrounding
the marble pools filled to the brim with cool, clear
water from the high cascading fountains. Even though a
month had gone by since she'd arrived back in the
country, she was still having considerable difficulty in
coming to terms with both the changes that had taken
place in Dhoman over the past years, and her own
emotional confusion about her relationship with her
husband.

Hussa hadn't been exaggerating when she had spoken
so enthusiastically concerning the sweeping reforms
which had been instituted by Badyr. During her first
week in the country, Leonie had become sharply aware
that there was an air of definite purpose, a new spirit
abroad in the country, with new industries, schools and
hospitals planned or being built in all the major towns.
Indeed, not content with simply razing the old palace
fortress to the ground, Badyr had also ordered the
bulldozing away of most of the decaying, decrepit
houses in Muria, replacing them with modern housing
estates and brand-new shopping centres.

One of the most astounding sights of all had been a
grand, spacious palace set on the waterfront of the
capital city. Badyr had told her that it was used mainly
for the formal entertainment and reception of important
guests, and was also the place where he held his *Majlis*.
This, she learned, was one of his innovations whereby,
once a week, any member of the population had the
right to see the Sultan.

'It may be that they are experiencing difficulties over

family matters, or wish me to settle a contentious dispute with a neighbour,' Badyr had explained. 'Whatever the problem, I feel that it is of prime importance that my people know that I care about them, and that they can always turn to me for help.'

Despite her resentment of the way she had been forced to return to Dhoman, each passing day had resulted in Leonie becoming more and more impressed both by Badyr's reforms, and by the obvious love and affection with which he was regarded by the populace.

Not that she'd been possessed of any such charitable thoughts that first evening after her arrival in the country. Staring silently down at her plate, she had been hardly able to eat any of the delicious food which had been placed in front of her, her whole being filled with deep anger against the man sitting on the other side of the table.

'Well, now . . .' Badyr had murmured as the servants poured the coffee and swiftly left the room. 'We must find something for you to do here in Dhoman, hmm?'

'I thought you'd already taken care of that!'

His only response to her bitter retort was a low, mocking laugh. 'Ah, my dear wife, although I might wish to spend all my waking hours pleasurably occupied with your delicious body . . . I'm afraid that I also have other matters to occupy my time. Alas, one must work as well as play, hmm?'

The urge to open her mouth and scream like a fishwife, telling him exactly what she thought about his notions of pleasure and play, was almost irresistible. Never had she felt so achingly tired and exhausted as she did at this moment, and no wonder, considering that she'd hardly been allowed out of bed all day! Desperately trying to banish the memory of his passionate lovemaking—and the humiliation of her own eager, feverish response—Leonie gritted her teeth as she struggled to control the flush spreading over her pale cheeks.

'Leaving aside your undoubted ... er ... wifely talents,' Badyr murmured with amusement, well aware of her suppressed fury, 'I also know that you are a competent businesswoman. And if you can run Dimitri Kashan's firm, then I am sure you will have no difficulty in organising some of the new projects I have in mind.'

'Such as . . .?'

'Such as the formation of a carpet and rug-making industry; and the setting up of a modern textile industry, concerned not only with producing the cloth but also with fabric design. Dhoman is one of the few places left in the world where the people still use indigo to dye material, for instance, and I thought you might be able to think of a way to make that a commercial proposition.'

Shocked out of her unhappy self-absorption, Leonie looked at him with bewilderment. 'I—I might be able to offer advice on marketing rugs, but Dhoman has no tradition of carpet-weaving. It's a marvellous idea, but it would take years to train the craftsmen needed, and I don't see how I could do that on my own. Besides, I haven't the slightest idea of how things are run in this country.'

'I have discovered that ruling a country requires exactly the same qualities as the management of a large firm,' Badyr said firmly. 'And I would not ask you to start organising new industries, badly needed in the outlying towns and villages, if I did not feel you were capable of doing so. You would have the support not only of myself and my ministers, but we would also make sure that adequate funds were made available as well as any technical advice you might require.'

Leonie stared blindly down at the table, aware of a rising tide of excitement. She could scarcely believe that Badyr meant what he said; that he wasn't going to insist on her spending her days shut away in the Harem. It seemed as if he really was going to give her the opportunity to do something useful with her life. There would be tremendous difficulties, of course, but what a challenge! Her euphoria was suddenly checked as she remembered that she was now living in Arabia.

'I—well, I think it's a wonderful idea, and I'd love to have the opportunity, but I don't see how it can work, I'm afraid. Being a woman in a Moslem country . . .' she gave a shrug of resignation. 'Well, you know the problems as well as I do.'

'I am not going to pretend that you won't occasionally experience difficulties, Leonie, but times have changed, certainly as far as Dhoman is concerned.' Badyr leaned back in his chair. 'Since becoming ruler, I have actively encouraged the return of all those of my countrymen who went to live abroad to escape my father's persecution, and there are also generous terms of employment for foreigners who have the necessary technical skills that we require.' He paused. 'I'm sure you'll be interested to know that we have also given asylum to a flood of refugees escaping from the war between Iran and Iraq—many of whom are carpet-weavers.'

'That's great! We could use their expertise, and . . .'

'Exactly!' Badyr smiled at her enthusiasm. 'Now, maybe you can see why I believe we can start a new carpet industry. And since many of the newcomers to this country have been used to living in more liberal areas of the world, I have relaxed the traditional rules regarding Moslem dress and habits. I am, in fact, hoping to promote a more *laissez-faire* rule in this country. Those who wish to keep to the old values are perfectly at liberty to do so, while modern dress, albeit reasonably discreet, is also freely permitted.'

'Is it working?'

'Most of the time. However, I am aware that I must make haste slowly if I am to unite my people into a cohesive whole, hmm? So, you will find that you are free to go about this country—always provided you will accept the presence of at least two guards, who will be there merely to protect you and not to pry on your business. Moreover, I am not expecting you to wear a veil, and when in our home I am happy to permit you to wear your own western clothes. Only on official occasions would I deem it a favour if you would dress in the discreet manner expected by our guests.'

Leonie hesitated, still trying to assimilate the fact that she was to be allowed some personal liberty, and the opportunity to do something positive. It all sounded far too good to be true—there must be a catch somewhere. 'Why didn't you tell me about all these reforms when we were in London?' she asked.

'Would you have believed me? Since you so firmly persist in regarding me as a wicked, lascivious villain, it would surely have been a waste of time, hmm?'

'Well, I . . . er . . .' She blushed, glancing up through her eyelashes to find Badyr's face creased into a broad smile. A smile of such intimate warmth and charm that she suddenly felt as if she had been stunned by a blow, leaving her feeling dazed and confused.

'I am still waiting for your answer,' he murmured as the silence lengthened between them. 'Are you willing to help me develop my country? Or is it a task for which you don't feel suitably qualified—something that is far beyond your mental and physical capabilities?'

'No—of course it isn't!' she retorted quickly, stung by his dismissive words, and also annoyed with herself for being so susceptible to his overwhelming masculinity.

'So, it is agreed. Excellent!' Badyr rose from the table.

'But there's so much to discuss . . . and I haven't exactly agreed to anything . . .' she protested breathlessly as he took her hand, leading her reluctant figure purposefully from the room and up the long, wide staircase to their suite.

'Oh, yes, you have, and I am quite confident that you will perform the services I require, to perfection.' He gave a low husky laugh as he closed their bedroom door. 'Just as certain as I am that you will perfectly perform the ... er ... service I require—tonight!'

And that had been that! Leonie thought with a wry smile as a clock chimed in the distance, reminding hter that she must get changed if she was to be ready on time for tonight's official banquet.

Walking through into the bedroom, she noted the shimmering white silk chiffon dress which Hussa had placed out ready for her to wear, its dramatic simplicity a perfect foil for the diamond tiara and matching necklace, glowing brilliantly in the velvet-lined casket set on an adjacent table. Leonie had long ceased to wonder why Badyr had bought up half of Bond Street, after she had set eyes on the fantastic clothes worn by most of the Arab women in Dhoman. Maryam and Badyr's half-sisters, Nadia and Sara, for instance, seemed to think nothing of having couture dresses flown over from Paris for special occasions, such as a wedding or a reception and banquet like that planned for tonight.

Slowly undressing, she frowned as she tried to think what to do about her relationship with Maryam, who had changed out of all recognition from the amusing child who had brightened Leonie's days in the grim old fortress. Now nineteen, Maryam had been oddly constrained on meeting her old friend again, and nothing Leonie could do seemed to be able to bridge the apparent gulf between them. It was obvious that Sheikh Samir was very attracted to Maryam—a feeling that was clearly reciprocated by the tall, slender girl— but that was surely no reason for her to be so awkward and nervous with her brother's wife?

Aside from wishing to resume her old companionship with Maryam, Leonie had been reluctant to have anything to do with Sultana Zenobia. However, she had eventually agreed to Badyr's request that she should pay a courtesy call on his mother. It hadn't, in fact, been quite as bad as she had feared, the older woman greeting her with far more cordiality than she had ever shown in the past, and clearly very taken with Jade.

'I do not blame you for hiding your pregnancy from me,' she had said with a bleak, wintry smile. 'We must all do what we think best for our children, something that you must realise by now, I think?' she added, the only time she had referred to the reason behind Leonie's forced return to Dhoman. 'I do hope, however, that you will permit your little daughter to visit me from time to time?'

Leonie had agreed, and Jade always seemed to have enjoyed herself when she returned from having tea with her formidable grandmother.

Sultana Fatima, on the other hand, was a complete contrast. Fatter than ever, she was clearly every bit as warm and jolly as she had always been. She would need all her good humour to put up with her daughter, Nadia, Leonie thought grimly. Now aged twenty-one, Nadia was a spoilt, selfish and discontented girl who was violently jealous of her younger sister, Sara.

It wasn't surprising that no one wanted to marry the shrewish Nadia, whereas Sara, a sweet girl with a soft, gentle personality, had been married for three years to Sheikh Hassan, the older of Badyr's two uncles. The elderly man, imprisoned by the old Sultan for protesting at Badyr's captivity, had been a widower with a young daughter at the time he had married Sara. They appeared to be very happy together with their young son, Ali, who was aged two and the present heir to Badyr's throne.

Leaving aside Hassan's daughter by his first wife, about whom Leonie knew nothing, the only other member of the family was Badyr's younger uncle, Feisal, whose whole life revolved around his precious Arab horses. He and Jade had taken to each other from the start—so much so that the little girl now practically lived in the stables!

Still thinking about Jade, Leonie went through into the bathroom and turned on the shower. Her daughter's obvious happiness in her new life, with a father she adored and her present love affair with her pony and her uncle Feisal, was ample proof that whatever her own problems, Leonie had chosen the right course of action. Not that Badyr had given her any real choice, of course, but she was glad—if only for Jade's sake—that she hadn't been tempted to run away from what she now saw to be her inevitable return to Dhoman.

The cool sting of the water was invigorating after the heat of the day, which had been spent wrestling with problems at one of the new textile mills. It was obviously going to take her a long time to put all Badyr's ideas into action, but already considerable progress had been made, especially with the Iranian exiles. They had been overjoyed to learn that their trade and ancient skills were valued in Dhoman, and several village workshops were in the course of construction.

Stepping out of the shower and towelling herself dry, she caught occasional glimpses of her pale body in the mirrored walls of the bathroom. Even her self-critical eyes couldn't help but notice the rich, silky sheen of her soft flesh, and the sparkling brilliance in her sapphire-blue eyes. There was no doubt that she had never looked better or more radiant in her life.

If she had initially hoped that Badyr's raging desire for her body would fade as the days went by, she soon found that she was doomed to disappointment. No matter how hard she had tried, no amount of firm resolution or downright refusal had any effect. Night after night there had been no reprieve, no respite from his passionate lovemaking.

At first, of course, she had fought him wildly, pummelling his broad shoulders with her clenched fists and kicking any part of his body that she could manage to reach. None of which had done her any good at all! The only response to her defiance had been

his low growls of sardonic amusement and a
contemptuous disregard of her violent, struggling figure
as his hands and mouth had worked their devilish
magic. How swiftly, how easily he had been able to turn
the protesting body in his arms into that of a pliant,
willing slave, moaning helplessly beneath his erotic,
sensual touch and eagerly crying out for his possession. Again and again he had demonstrated his
power over her, and after the first few nights, Leonie
had been forced to ask herself who she was fighting . . .
Badyr or her own emotions? That question now, of
course, seemed merely an academic exercise. There was
no point in continually asking herself how she could
respond so ardently to Badyr—a man who had not only
treated her shamefully, but had also blackmailed her
into returning to Dhoman. The shocking truth was . . .
she no longer cared!

It had taken her a long time, but she could now
acknowledge the fact that, despite all that had
happened, she had never stopped loving the man she
had first met when she was only eighteen. She still
didn't understand how Badyr could have virtually
deserted her for so many years. Perhaps she never
would. However, everything in the past now seemed
somehow irrelevant, when set beside the deep feelings
she had for the only man she had ever loved. It wasn't
just the physical side of their relationship, the driving
need to possess each other which seemed to increase in
intensity with each passing day. Working together for
the good of the country, she and Badyr had forged new
bonds of warmth and friendship. She admired his
selfless devotion to his people, his care and concern that
they should have a better life. She was also irresistibly
drawn to the inner kindness beneath the hard, forceful
and ruthless personality with which he faced the world.
She loved him with all her heart—for his faults as well
as his virtues—and that was the beginning and end of it
as far as her own emotions were concerned.

But what about Badyr? He was more than frank about his physical need for her, a fact clearly demonstrated by the nights they spent locked in each other's arms. But he had been ominously silent about his deeper feelings. When Badyr had assured her mother that he had always loved her ... had he ... could he have been speaking the truth? Leonie sighed. She must be realistic. As much as she wanted to, it would be folly to forget the long years of silence after she had left Dhoman, foolish to ignore the fact that she was only here because she had refused to leave her daughter. And yet ...

Her heart heavy with longing for what could never be, Leonie leant weakly against the cool mirrored surface of the wall for a moment, before slipping into a silk dressing-gown and trailing slowly back into the bedroom. She was so preoccupied with her thoughts that it was a few seconds before she realised she wasn't alone. Badyr, who had been standing by the windows, turned at her entry, his dark eyes gleaming with amusement as he removed his black patch and tossed it aside.

'I have just been having a long talk with Jade. I have told her that she must be a good girl while we are away for a few days.'

Leonie looked at him with startled eyes. 'What on earth are you talking about?'

'I have decided to visit my summer palace in the south of the country. We won't be away for very long, and Jade will be perfectly happy with Miss Jackson and my uncle Feisal.'

'But I can't possibly leave at the moment. The new textile mill is having real difficulties, and ...'

'While I am full of admiration for all you have done over the past month, it is useless for you to argue with me. We are going to have a break for a few days—and that is the end of the matter,' he said bluntly.

Leonie sighed heavily. It was futile to try and oppose

him once he had made up his mind, but she could hardly bear to think about the problems she would have to face when they returned. Despite all the help given to her by Badyr and his Minister of Development, the new manager of the mill—like every other Arab man with whom she dealt—did not take kindly to being given orders by a woman.

'Jade didn't take the news of our departure very well, either,' Badyr laughed. 'I now know the meaning of perpetual energy—it is undoubtedly her tongue!'

'I did warn you,' she muttered, going over to her chest of drawers to select some frothy silk underwear.

'So you did,' he agreed, swiftly undoing his wide gold belt and stepping out of the loose robes he habitually wore when in Dhoman. Crossing the marble floor towards Leonie, who was standing with her back to him, he slowly ran a finger down her spine. 'I can also remember you saying that you would never—ever—willingly submit to me, hmm?'

It was as if she was paralysed, unable to move or speak as he gently brushed aside the long length of her curly hair, softly pressing his lips to her neck. An icy shiver feathered down her backbone and she was powerless to resist the hands that moved to untie her belt, slowly edging the silk gown from off her shoulders to let it fall in a pool at her feet as he turned and drew her trembling, naked figure to rest against his hard body.

'Well, Leonie?' he murmured thickly, not waiting for an answer as he lowered his dark head to lightly brush her lips with his mouth, the kiss filling her senses with such an aching sweetness that her lips quivered and parted, a soft moan breaking from her throat as her arms crept slowly up to encircle his neck.

He slowly withdrew his mouth, gazing down into the blue eyes cloudy with desire, before giving a low laugh and sweeping her up into his arms to carry her with effortless ease towards the bed.

'No, Badyr, we can't . . .!' she gasped as he intimately caressed her trembling body.

'Oh, yes we can, my beloved,' he breathed huskily, his mouth causing havoc with her senses as it captured first one rosy peak of her breasts and then another.

'But the reception and banquet, and the guests?'

'Without my presence there can be no reception or banquet. So, our guests will just have to await my pleasure, hmm? And since, darling one, my pleasure is to be found here with you at this moment—in the possession of your delicious, quite irresistible body—there is no more to be said!'

They were indeed late, arriving at the reception a good half-hour after all the guests had assembled. Badyr blandly proffered his apologies without bothering to give an adequate excuse, but Leonie suspected that anyone looking at her flushed face and heightened colouring would be in no doubt as to *exactly* what had delayed them. And after receiving a beaming smile from the charming French Ambassador, she was certain of the fact!

She was still feeling embarrassed about the episode, and unhappy about leaving Jade, when she returned later with Badyr to their palace.

'Save your breath!' he said, with an infuriating, mocking smile as he stood aside to allow her to stalk ahead into their bedroom. 'I have not forgotten that it took me two whole weeks to persuade you to leave London! That was a quite exhausting experience which I certainly have no intention of repeating. Now, let us hear no more of the matter. It is time we were in bed and asleep.'

'The day you get into bed and go straight off to sleep, will be the day I drop dead with shock!' she snapped.

'Ah, my poor darling, I cannot face the responsibility of causing you such a sad end,' he laughed, walking over to take her into his arms. 'I can see that I must

make the ultimate sacrifice, and save you from tha
terrible fate, hmm?' he added, removing her tiara and
casually tossing the priceless diamonds into a nearby
chair.

'*Oh, you're impossible!*' She glared at him, her hear
beginning to thud as she glimpsed the naked desire in
the dark eyes gleaming down at her. ' "The ultimat
sacrifice"—indeed! You've got a nerve!' she muttered
huskily as he plucked out the combs from her hair
trying not to respond to his warm, sensual smile. 'Yo
know what you are, don't you? You're ... you're
absolutely and utterly ... incorrigible!' she gasped
weakly surrendering to the demanding arousal of th
mouth that descended to possess her trembling lips.

Leonie sat out on the wide terrace of the Summe
Palace, gazing out over the rolling waves of the greeny
blue sea to the wide, empty horizon where the Arabia
Sea mingled with the waters of the Indian Ocean. Th
sun was just setting, the fiery glow turning the long
sandy beach into a ribbon of deep, rich amber as i
wound its way through the palm trees in the coconu
groves along the shore-line.

She had been astounded to find that instead of th
vast, sandy desert of her imagination, the province o
Mazun was an entrancing surprise. Covering an are
about the size of Wales, high mountain ranges formed
half-circle to enclose a green crescent-shaped, fertil
plain bordered by long miles of sandy beaches tha
would make most Caribbean islanders weep with envy
Badyr had explained that by some strange quirk o
climate, monsoons just touched this corner of Arabia
lasting from June to September every year.

'The bad news is that during the monsoon, the coas
is covered in cloud and fog. It never seems to stop
raining, and much of the province becomes a muddy
cold, insect-ridden land of dark, murky gloom!'

His lips curved into a broad smile. 'However, th

good news, my dear Leonie,' he continued, 'is that for the rest of the year, Mazun is warm, green and overflowing with semi-tropical vegetation. Rivers flow through fields of wheat, sugar cane and cotton; mountain streams gurgle their way past groves of coconut palms; the sea is blue, the beaches are golden and it is for me—and I hope for you, also—a land of milk and honey!'

From what she had seen of the province during the drive from the airport yesterday, Leonie could easily understand why Badyr had spoken so poetically about this particular area of Dhoman. The green fields had seemed to be full of abundant crops and the meadows filled with flowers and herds of fat browsing cattle.

Standing amidst lush gardens and directly on the seashore, the Summer Palace was a long turreted building, surrounded by and hidden behind high walls. Inside the building, which had been built by Badyr's great-grandfather, Sultan Karim, in the late eighteen-seventies, a maze of inter-connecting courtyards and alley-ways led to rooms of differing architectural styles.

'This really is a lovely place,' she said, smiling up at Badyr as he joined her on the terrace, followed by servants bringing coffee and flickering lamps that glowed in the gathering dusk. 'Has it been in your family for a long time?'

'Every Sultan since Karim's time has fallen in love with the province and this palace,' Badyr said. 'And every one of them has added a room here, or a complete wing there. I was born here, and one way and another I seem to have spent a considerable amount of time in this building.' His lips twisted into a grim smile.

'Was this where . . .?'

'Yes,' he answered her hesitant enquiry. 'This is where my father had me confined after my arrest. It seems very pleasant, doesn't it? But I can assure you that after experiencing two monsoons during my incarceration here, if I hadn't managed to escape, I

would have undoubtedly shot myself from sheer gloom
and depression!'

Although he had spoken the words lightly, the bleak
underlying tone in his voice was unmistakable. There
was a long pause as he leaned back in his chair staring
blindly out into space.

'I have very ambivalent feelings about this lovely
place,' he said at last. 'Maybe that is natural, since no
one would willingly choose to return to their old jail.
Redecorating and refurbishing the rooms has helped, of
course, but nevertheless ...' He sighed deeply and fell
silent, only the sounds of the sea lapping against the
sand disturbing the still night air.

Leonie sat quietly, hardly daring to move in case she
disturbed his train of thought. For so long she had
wondered what had happened to Badyr after his arrest,
and now, at last, it seemed that he might be going to fill
in some of the missing pieces of the jigsaw puzzle.

'I was brought down here under heavy guard, right in
the middle of a torrential downpour that seemed to last
for months!' he said wryly. 'The place was devoid of
any human inhabitants—other than myself and my
guards, of course. The only benefit of such solitary
confinement was that I had a great deal of time in
which to think about what I wanted to do for my
country, and how to implement the plans I had made. I
must confess that it would not have been too difficult to
escape. However,' he shrugged his shoulders, 'my father
put paid to that notion—rather cleverly, I thought.'

'He ... he told me,' Leonie murmured. 'He said he
would put me in a dungeon if you even so much as
talked to anyone, let alone tried to escape. I ... I'm
sorry, Badyr, there wasn't anything I could do to help
you.'

'My dear girl!' he smiled. 'My father was so firmly in
the grip of senile dementia by that time, that not even
all the luscious, shapely houris in paradise could have
prevailed upon his crazed senses! Nevertheless, it

became increasingly obvious I must escape before the country became engulfed in a civil war—my father versus the entire population!—but I had to see to your safety before I made the attempt.'

'You said, in London, that you had arranged for me to leave the country. But, I thought your mother . . .?'

'Let us just say that she and I came to an arrangement,' he remarked flatly, a muscle tightening along his jaw. 'Not one that I would ever normally have agreed to—but I was not in a position that allowed me any choice in the matter.' With a heavy sigh, Badyr rose from his chair to pace silently up and down the dark terrace.

'How I wish . . .' he muttered under his breath, and then gave a harsh laugh. 'If wishes were horses, beggars would ride! There is nothing to be gained by bitterly regretting what is already history in the sands of time. What is done is done, hmm?'

'Yes, yes, I suppose so,' Leonie murmured, totally confused by the underlying savage tone in his voice, and not having the least idea of what he was talking about. 'But you haven't told me how you escaped, or . . .'

'We will leave that for another time. It is growing late and I'm sure you will agree that there are far more important things we have to talk about.'

Leonie peered up at his tall figure, silhouetted against the light of the rising moon. Badyr seemed in such a strange mood tonight, and she couldn't for the life of her think what . . .

His low voice interrupted her confused thoughts. 'Just why do you think that I wanted us to be alone together? You have been in Dhoman for over a month now, and it is surely time that we discussed our relationship.' He came over to stand before her looking down at her pale face lit by the moonlight. 'Can you tell me that it is not passionate desire that you feel in my arms each night?' he said softly. 'Can you deny the soft, tremulous cries of pleasure that haunt my days like a siren's song, calling me back to your sweet body night after night?'

Leonie shook her head, shivering in the cool night air. She couldn't seem to find her voice, but neither could she deny or repudiate any of the things he said.

'Has it occurred to you that, in time, such feelings might become more than a purely physical response?' he asked gently. 'That you might possibly be able to forget the past, and learn to love me again—as I love and have always loved you? Or have my actions in the past destroyed all chance of that happening?'

Leonie gazed up at him, her mind and senses whirling in chaotic disbelief at what she was hearing. Was Badyr really saying ...? It didn't seem possible, and yet ... Her heart began a wild pounding, the blood surging and racing through her veins as her mouth suddenly became dry and she swallowed nervously, almost feeling sick with rising excitement.

'I ... er ... could you p-possibly repeat w-what you've just s-said,' she stammered helplessly.

'Ah, my darling,' he murmured, drawing her up into his arms and burying his face in the fragrant cloud of her hair. 'I never stopped loving you, never for one minute of my life. I know ...' he added as she stirred restlessly in his embrace, 'I have treated you abominably. First in not telling you the entire truth about what you would find when you first came to Dhoman, and then, when you had escaped from the Harem, in not contacting you for so long.'

He put his hands on her arms, holding her away from him and staring intently down at her bemused expression. 'Love is very much a matter of trust, hmm? So, I am asking you to trust me, my dearest one. I would not have deserted you, other than for your own sweet sake. Please believe me when I say that I could not leave Dhoman, and it was only because I wished everything to be absolutely right for you, that I did not bring you back here any sooner. I loved you too much to do that. Can you understand that I made what I felt to be the best decision—in your own interests?'

'I don't really understand anything you've been saying, except . . .' She paused. 'You do really love me?'

'Oh, my darling, how can you doubt it!' he whispered thickly, cupping her lovely face in his hands. 'I would never have stolen Jade from you. But when I realised that you had been so hurt, so disillusioned by my desertion that you would not return to Dhoman, I had no alternative but to blackmail you into returning to this country. I have lived in desperate hope that your love for me was not dead, that given time it would come back to life and flower once again.'

'Oh, Badyr,' she breathed huskily.

The next instant she was locked tightly in his arms as he rained fervent kisses on her upturned face. Her heart leapt for joy as all her doubts and uncertainties dissolved and vanished away. Dizzy with the almost unbelievably wonderful fact that Badyr loved her, she wound her arms about his neck, drawing him closer to her trembling body as his hands slid sensuously over her warm curves; aware of his quickening desire and that his heartbeat was as rapid as her own.

'My darling Badyr. I never stopped loving you!' she whispered softly.

With a strangled cry of triumph, he swept her up in his arms. Carrying her as if she weighed no more than thistledown, he strode across the terrace and into the palace, swiftly mounting the stairs two at a time until he reached their bedroom where he laid her on the downy softness of the large bed.

'My beloved Leonie, I have such a great, over-powering love for you,' he murmured, quickly stripping off his clothes before slowly removing the light caftan she was wearing. His long, tanned fingers moved caressingly over her pale skin, casting aside the thin scraps of silk and lace as he exposed her full naked beauty.

'Exquisite!' he breathed thickly, his hands erotically stroking the full ripe curves and thrusting peaks of her breasts and the tender softness of her stomach. Leonie's flesh trembled beneath his touch, a sense of wild exultation at the intensity of his desire flowing through her veins like quicksilver. As if under a magic spell, she floated in a dreamlike trance as Badyr's lovemaking raised her to peaks of ecstasy she had never attained before, sweeping her up in a wild spiral of ever-escalating rapture until, when she was certain she could not bear the deliriously exciting agony a moment longer, his body merged with hers in a heavenly explosion of joyous, rapturous delight.

The long hot days and nights merged together into a shining stream of delight and happiness. It was as if Leonie and Badyr were discovering a completely new world together, one that was encompassed by the high walls surrounding the Summer Palace. Wandering hand in hand through the many rooms, or lying out under the shady trees in a garden full of the scent of exotic flowers, Leonie revelled in the beauty that surrounded her on every side.

'They are nothing to *your* ravishing beauty, my dearest,' Badyr murmured drowsily one hot afternoon as Leonie called his attention to the brilliant, shimmering colours of a pair of humming-birds hovering over a small pool of crystal clear water, near where they were lying on the grass.

'Oh Badyr—do look! Aren't they lovely?'

'I am looking.' He raised himself up on one elbow, leaning over her prone figure as his fingers moved to slowly untie her long, filmy gown, sliding it off her shoulders and exposing the unconfined, sweet curves of her breasts. 'And they are indeed lovely!' he breathed, his eyes savouring her beauty before he bent to touch his lips first to one rosy peak and then the other.

An echo of the previous night's lovemaking rippled

through her body and she uttered a shivering sigh of deep pleasure. 'I can't believe that I can be so happy!'

'Umm,' he murmured, his erotic kiss deepening as his mouth teased her nipples until she gave a small cry of pain. 'Darling?' he looked at her with concern. 'I did not mean to hurt you.'

'No, you didn't, not really. It's just—well, I'm a bit sensitive at the moment. I wasn't sure until a few days ago, but . . .' She paused, suddenly feeling oddly nervous. 'I think . . . in fact, I'm quite sure—that I'm going to have a baby.'

If she had been worried about his reaction to the news, her fears were instantly put at rest by his overwhelming joy and pleasure at the news. 'You wonderful, wonderful woman!' he exclaimed, clasping her rapturously in his arms. 'And I promise you, my darling,' he murmured later as he tenderly stroked her warm flesh, 'that I will be close beside you at all times during your pregnancy. I cannot ever forgive myself for not being by your side when you were expecting Jade.' He smiled tenderly down at the girl in his arms. 'We shall call him Karim, after my great-grandfather.'

Leonie laughed. '"Him" . . .? Well, I don't recommend buying the baby a train-set just yet—*she* might prefer to play with a doll!'

'Oh no,' he said, his hands moving possessively over her stomach. 'You are going to give me a son to rule this land after me. Of that I am quite certain!'

'And . . . and if I don't? If it should happen to be a little girl?' she asked, her blue eyes suddenly shadowed by uncertainty.

'Ah, my dearest, I will then have the perfect excuse— if I am ever likely to need one!—to keep on making love to you until we have a great tribe of children.' He lowered his head to passionately kiss her lips. 'Yes, of course I want a son, but if Allah should bless us with another daughter—like my little Jade—then I will be more than happy and content.'

Reassured by his words, Leonie surrendered to the tide of desire engendered by his lips and hands, the long lean length of his hard body as he swiftly removed their clothes. She gloried in the intimate contact of his warm flesh against her yielding softness, the throbbing urgency of his arousal as unable to contain himself, he possessed her there and then on the soft green grass. Only her small moans of excitement disturbed the peaceful setting, the high afternoon sun slanting down through the tall trees to cast long, golden shadows on the figures which lay so closely and intimately entwined together on the green lawn far below.

CHAPTER SEVEN

'ALAS, all good things must come to an end—if only temporarily,' Badyr said with a wry smile as they sat together at breakfast one morning. 'I'm afraid that I have no choice, my darling, but to begin a round of official duties, which means that my uncle Hassan will be joining us tomorrow.'

Leonie sighed. She was still so emotionally caught up in the wonder and delight of Badyr's love, that she resented anyone or anything that interrupted their blissful reunion.

'Besides, you will want to see Jade again. You said last night that talking to her on the radio-telephone was not very satisfactory.'

'No, it wasn't, but at least I needn't worry about her having missed us too much. It sounds as if your uncle Feisal is absolutely her favourite man of the moment. If you don't watch out, you won't be "stu-pen-dous" any more!'

'Where on earth does she pick up these words?' he asked, his mouth twitching with amusement.

'Think yourself lucky! Three months ago, she heard something on the television and it was weeks before my mother and I could stop her shouting "for-nic-ation", at the top of her voice!' Leonie giggled.

Badyr threw back his head and roared with laughter. 'I am sorry, my darling, but I think I really must pray very hard to ensure that our coming child is indeed a boy. Can you imagine what it would be like to have two little daughters like Jade? *Wallahi!* I do not think I could stand the ... er ... strain!'

'I hadn't thought of that,' Leonie agreed with a smile.

'Oh, by the way,' he added as he rose from the table.

'It occurred to me that it might be nice for Jade to get to know her little cousin, Ali. So I have invited not only my uncle Hassan, but his wife and son also. You will be pleased to see Sara again, yes?'

'Yes, of course. Although Ali's only two, and just a little young for Jade, who will probably order him around unmercifully,' she smiled. 'I'm very fond of your half-sister, who's every bit as sweet and placid as her mother.'

'We must hope that Sara does not become *quite* as fat as Fatima—my stepmother seems to grow more enormous with every passing day!'

But there seemed no likelihood of that, Leonie thought, as she sat out on the terrace one afternoon a few days later. Sara was still slim and petite, although she had confessed with a shy smile that she was expecting another baby in seven months' time.

'And, maybe you, too?' Sara had murmured that morning, casting a knowing eye over Leonie's glowing skin and the burgeoning swell of her breasts beneath the long filmy gown.

Leonie had wanted to keep her pregnancy a precious secret between Badyr and herself, until such time as it became too obvious to hide. But Sara's unexpectedly shrewd question had caught her on the hop, and she had not been able to hide her blushing, tell-tale confusion.

Now, as Sara's little boy, Ali, played quietly in the sand by the edge of the terrace, she asked Sara not to tell anyone else about the coming baby.

'I feel it's terribly important that Jade hears about the new baby from Badyr and myself, and doesn't pick it up from a servant's careless remark. Although, you know what the gossip in these palaces is like,' she added drily. 'Everyone knows exactly what is going on, weeks before one knows it oneself!'

'Very true!' Sara agreed ruefully. 'But where is little Jade? I have not seen her all afternoon.'

'When Badyr's uncle Feisal invited your husband and mine to go fishing on his yacht, Jade gave him no peace until she was allowed to go too!' Leonie laughed. 'I think Feisal invited Elizabeth Jackson along simply to make sure he retained his sanity!'

'Well,' Sara mused. 'That may be so, but I think Feisal likes Miss Jackson very much. In fact, I wouldn't be at all surprised . . .' She hesitated.

'Oh, no—surely not?' Leonie looked at her with startled eyes. 'He's far too old for Elizabeth! I mean . . .' she paused, horrified by what she had said as she realised that Sara's husband, Hassan, was considerably older than his brother, Feisal.

'Relax, Leonie!' Sara smiled. 'You have an expression in England, do you not? "There is many a good tune played on an old fiddle"! Hassan may have grey hair, but I can assure you that my dear husband is very . . . er . . . very vigorous in every other respect!' she giggled.

'For the love of Allah—can't you two talk about anything else but marriage and babies?'

Leonie bit back a sharp retort as she looked over at the girl lounging on one of the comfortable chairs spread along the terrace. She hadn't been pleased to find that Nadia had invited herself along to the Summer Palace with Sara and her husband, and the girl's malicious, bitter comments were beginning to get under her skin.

'Marriage and babies are a fact of life—literally!' she murmured with a smiling shrug of her shoulders.

'Babies! We poor women find ourselves trapped as soon as we marry!'

Leonie gave a light laugh, attempting to defuse the situation as Sara's small figure bristled in the chair beside her. 'That may possibly be true, Nadia. But when you fall in love, you will undoubtedly find that you are happy to be caught in such a warm, tender trap!'

'*Never!*' Nadia cast a spiteful glance at the English

girl's fair, glowing beauty. 'You may be fool enough to welcome your husband straight from his other wife's bed, but I would never submit to such an indignity!'

'Oh, for heaven's sake! What on earth are you talking about?' Leonie looked at her in puzzlement, only half aware of Sara's hands fluttering in the air as she tried to prevent her sister from saying any more.

'Oh, it's all so stupid!' Nadia snapped at Sara. 'I ask you—how does Badyr think he can possibly keep Leonie from hearing about Aisha? She's bound to find out sooner or later. Surely it's better that she knows the truth?'

'*Nadia!* How can you do this?' Sara cried, jumping to her feet in consternation. 'Badyr will *kill* you! Why must you take such delight in being malicious and cruel?'

'I don't understand.' Leonie looked on in confusion as the two sisters began screaming at each other in Arabic. 'W-what "other wife"? And who is Aisha? I've never heard of her, I . . .'

'Of course you haven't—you poor fool!' Nadia spat the words venomously. 'Your precious husband is no better than any other man. He wants to have his cake and eat it too, doesn't he? Oh, yes,' she gave a wild laugh, 'Badyr's certainly a good Moslem. You should think yourself fortunate, Leonie, that he's only got *one* other wife—he's allowed up to four at any one time, you know!'

Leonie couldn't move. She sat stunned by Nadia's words, not able to comprehend what the other girl was saying. Badyr—married to another woman? Another wife? It couldn't possibly be true. Nadia was just trying to make even more trouble than usual—of course she was! The very idea was too extraordinarily foolish and far-fetched to be worth taking seriously. She'd have to tell Badyr to send Nadia back to her mother as soon as possible. She really wasn't going to put up with any more of the girl's stupid, malicious remarks.

Leonie turned to Sara, shocked to see the girl sitting slumped in her chair with tears streaming down her cheeks. 'For goodness sake, there's no need to cry! Nadia's just being silly, that's all . . .' Her voice died away as Sara turned to look at her, the expression of sorrow and pity in her eyes sending shivers of fear down her spine.

'Yes, it is true,' Sara whispered, agitatedly hunting for a handkerchief to wipe her eyes. 'Oh, Leonie, I am so . . . so sorry. I know that such customs are difficult for western women to understand. But I also know that my brother does love you very much, and . . .'

'But how, why?' Leonie felt cold, icy fingers tightening around her heart. 'And who is Aisha?'

Sara glared over at Nadia, who was sitting back in her chair with a smirk on her face. 'You had better start saying your prayers, you wicked, wicked girl. Because when Badyr finds out what you have done, he will surely tear you limb from limb!' she ground out through clenched teeth.

'For God's sake, Sara, tell me the truth!' Leonie cried, as Nadia merely responded to her sister's words with a defiant toss of her dark head. She suddenly felt desperately sick, and tight bands seemed to be closing about her ribs making it difficult for her to breathe.

Sara gave an unhappy sigh and fiercely blew her nose. 'Badyr swore us all to secrecy . . . but yes, it is true. You see,' she shrugged her shoulders, 'it is traditional in our family for the eldest son to marry his uncle's daughter. Feisal is not married, and so—as expected—Badyr married his young cousin Aisha, the daughter of his uncle, Hassan. I hope you can understand—it is maybe a little complicated.' Sara looked at the English girl with compassion.

'But *you* are married to Hassan.' Leonie shook her head in stunned confusion.

'Aisha's mother died of tuberculosis soon after she was born; a disease that has killed many of her family

in the past,' Sara explained. 'It was only after many
years, long after his daughter Aisha was married to
Badyr, that I married Hassan.

'But how? I mean ... where? And when?' Leonie
whispered.

'I do not know all the details, since I was much
younger at the time.' The other girl sighed heavily.
'However, I think it was over five years ago that they
were married, and she now lives up in the mountains
behind Muria. But, Leonie, it is important that you
understand.'

What it was important that she understand, Leonie
never heard, the full horror of her situation scorching
through her trembling body like a blinding flash of
lightning. As her brain struggled to comprehend the
terrible fact that not only was she bigamously married
to Badyr, but that her precious little daughter was
illegitimate, something seemed to snap in her brain. The
terrace, the palace and the sea beyond began to spin,
revolving faster and faster and drawing her down into a
swirling void. The last sound she heard was her own
strangled moan as she lost all hold of reality, limply
falling out of the chair on to the hard stone terrace.

Leonie surfaced from the swirling mists, gazing
blindly about her in dazed confusion as she dimly
realised she was lying on her bed. The room itself
seeming to be filled with a crowded mass of servants, all
shrieking at the tops of their voices. A moment later,
Sara's worried face swam before her eyes, bending over
Leonie's prone body to place a cold cloth on her brow.
The noise and confusion suddenly seemed too much for
her to cope with, a low moan breaking from her lips as
she slipped thankfully back into the darkness once
more.

When she finally returned to full consciousness, all
the noise and confusion had disappeared. Looking
around she saw that the room was empty, save for
Badyr's tall figure pacing distractedly up and down by

the tall windows. She couldn't prevent a strangled gasp of horror as she began to recall the scene on the terrace, the sound bringing Badyr instantly to her side.

'What has happened to you, my dearest?' he murmured, sitting down beside her on the bed. 'I can get no sense from anyone in this palace! When I returned from the yachting trip, it was to find Sara in floods of tears and refusing to explain matters, the servants hiding in their quarters and wailing as if there had been a death in the family—and all I have been able to gather is that you fainted out on the terrace. So, please tell me what is wrong, darling,' he added, softly brushing the hair away from her brow.

The warm, gentle touch of his hand was almost more than she could bear, the tears welling up to trickle down her cheeks in a steady stream.

'Ah, my sweet, my dear one. I have called for a doctor, and we will soon have you well again.'

'I'll never—ever—be well again!' She turned her head away, burying her face in the pillows, her slim figure racked with sobs.

'Come, this is foolish, Leonie. You have no need to weep.'

'Haven't I?' she moaned. She felt as cold as death although her body was shaking as if in the grip of a raging fever. 'What do you expect me to do when I find out that my husband is a lying, cheating adulterer, and that my child is . . . is a bastard!'

The hands that had been gently stroking her hair became suddenly still, and the faint hope that Nadia and Sara were mistaken—that it was, after all, only a bad dream, a nightmare—drained away in the long silence that followed her tortured cry of anguish.

'It's true, isn't it? You really do have another wife?' she whispered, her hoarse voice echoing around the room as she struggled to sit up.

Leonie's dazed blue eyes stared fixedly at Badyr, noting the blood draining from his face to leave it pale and strained beneath his tan, the deepening lines about his hard, firm lips. It was as if he had been turned to stone, only a vein beating furiously in his temple giving any indication of his inner tension.

'Well?' Her trembling, shaking hand dashed away the tears which were beginning to fall again. *'Have you—or have you not—another wife?'* she demanded harshly.

Badyr gave a deep, heavy sigh, putting his hand to his forehead for a moment as if in pain. 'Yes, Leonie. I cannot deny, however much I might wish to do so, that I have another wife. But . . .'

'But—*nothing!* Or maybe Nadia's right?' she gave a wild, hysterical laugh. 'Maybe you've got at least four of us "wives" stashed away around the country?'

'Nadia!' he suddenly roared, rising swiftly to his feet and striding about the room. 'I might have known that little bitch . . .'

'She may be a bitch—but she was absolutely right!' Leonie cried, anger coming to the aid of her stunned mind as a torrent of rage flowed through her body. 'For God's sake! Just how long did you think you could keep me in blissful ignorance? Someone was bound to tell me that I'm . . . I'm . . . God knows what I am! Some s-sort of c-c-concubine . . .?' she wailed, throwing herself down on the pillows again in a paroxysm of hysterical tears.

Badyr strode swiftly over to the bed and gathered her weeping figure into his arms. 'Oh, my dearest, my beloved one. You are indeed my true wife, that I assure you. And our child is not a bastard! I promise you that she is legally my daughter, as our son will be also.'

'You *promise* me? Your promises don't mean a damn thing!' she cried, wrenching herself away from his embrace. 'And what's "legal" mean in this bloody country, anyway? It's legal for a man to have four wives at one and the same time, and all his children are legal—whoever their mother might be. But . . . but you just try living your so-called legal way of life in Europe or the United States . . . and you'd soon find yourself locked up for bigamy! They'd shove you into jail so fast, that even your handsome head would be spinning like a top!'

Badyr rose to stride agitatedly about the room. 'I assure you, Leonie, that you are my first, my legal wife. I give you my solemn promise that our marriage will stand examination in any European or American court. It therefore follows that Jade is my true daughter, and that the child you carry is definitely not a bastard.'

'*Big deal!* Thanks a million!' she lashed back furiously. 'And what about all your other wives and their children? What do you tell them? A version of the same bedtime story you've just given me. God . . .! *I can't believe this is happening to me!*' Her cry of pain and anguish echoed around the room, reverberating in her ears like the knell of doom.

'Leonie! I beg you to be calm.'

'Calm? Did you say *calm*!' she screamed, rising from the bed. 'I'll give you "calm", *my fine Sultan*!' she hissed, swiftly raising her hand to give him a resounding slap on his tanned cheek.

'Enough!' he commanded curtly, catching hold of her wrist as she aimed another retaliatory blow at his face. 'I can understand your wish to hit me, but it will achieve nothing.'

'Don't you believe it!' she panted, trying to break away from his iron grip. 'If I had a knife in my hands, I'd plunge it into your black heart without a moment's hesitation!'

His lips twisted wryly. 'Ah, yes, my vixen—I can readily believe that you would.'

'It's no laughing matter!'

'I agree,' he said in a flat, heavy voice, bending swiftly to seize hold of her struggling body. 'Now, we must talk sensibly and calmly, yes?' he murmured as he carried her over to the bed, before sitting down beside her and gripping her hands tightly together between his own.

'I had married no other woman before you, and our marriage is perfectly legal—both here in Arabia and in the Western world. That is the first point I wish to make. Yes, I do have another wife, whom I married according to Moslem law—*after* our marriage—and that is also a legal marriage as far as she and I are concerned. Do you understand me, Leonie?' He grasped hold of her chin, holding it steady as he forced her to meet his dark, troubled gaze.

'Oh, I understand all right!' Her voice wobbled dangerously as she fought to control her pain and anguish. 'I clearly understand that you seem to think that because I was the first of your . . . your paramours, that makes everything just fine and dandy! God—what a swine you are! How many other wives and children have you got—or isn't it polite of me to ask?'

'I have only one other wife, and no children other than Jade,' he replied evenly. 'I know you may not believe me. However, if you consider the matter, you will see that while I have indeed been guilty of the sin of omission, I have never deliberately lied to you.'

'Your definition of the word "lie" and mine are hardly likely to agree, are they?' she grated bitterly. 'As far as I'm concerned the last five years has been one big lie on your part, not to mention that little item: for-nic-ation!'

'My darling, if you would just listen to me.'

'And give you a chance to sweet-talk me into accepting this revolting, bizarre set-up? Forget it! And while I'm on the subject of "sweet-talk", have you bothered to tell your other wife about me? Or have you kept her ignorant of my existence too?'

'No, of course not. Aisha knows all about you, and . . .'

Leonie gasped, nearly choking on the hard lump of dark jealousy which seemed to fill her throat. 'What a

jolly little *ménage à trois!*' She gave a cracked laugh.
'I'm sure you've both had a lot of fun discussing me—
been seeing a lot of her lately, have you?'

Badyr stared at her for a moment, his face white and
strained. 'Yes, Leonie,' he said quietly. 'I've had to. But
I've never . . .'

'*Wow!* You're quite the sexual athlete, aren't you?'
She began to laugh, and found she couldn't stop. The
crazy, shrill tones echoed around the room until Badyr
raised his hand and gave her a quick slap on the face.

'I'm sorry, my darling! I had to do it,' he whispered
as she hiccuped into silence, staring bleakly at him with
eyes that were deep blue pools of misery. 'Please stop
torturing yourself—and me—so unnecessarily.'

'Oh, Badyr . . .' Leonie shook her head helplessly.
'Why on earth did you drag me away from my life in
London? How . . . how could you be so cruel to make
me go through this agony? Why, why?' She stared at
him, the blood draining from her face. 'Oh, no! *What a
fool I've been!*' she groaned, stiffening with shock and
almost paralysed as she was struck by the horrifying
truth.

'It's because you need a son, isn't it? Oh, God—I can
see it all now! Your precious Aisha hasn't given you
any children—and so what do you do? You look
around and suddenly remember the girl who was so
foolish as to marry you, and whom you've completely
forgotten about for the last five years. After all, you got
me pregnant fast enough, didn't you? Since Aisha
hasn't come up trumps—why not put stupid old Leonie
in the family way? She might be a bit of a nuisance—
but at least she's fertile! Right, Badyr?'

'For God's sake, *no!*'

Leonie gave him a savage, mocking grimace of a
smile, her voice harsh with loathing and disgust as she
ignored his sharp protest.

'Wait a bit—the story's just beginning to get
interesting! Using his considerable talents . . . mostly

trickery, blackmail and a lot of oily, sexy charm . . . our handsome hero manages to haul the silly woman back to Dhoman. And guess what? Yes, fast as knife, she conceives a baby! And—now this really is the clever bit—*it's all as legal as can be*! Ho, ho! Our hero is laughing like a drain, isn't he? He's got his second wife, whom he's been happily living with for the last five years, *and* someone else to have his children. Clever . . . c-clever B-B-Badyr . . .!' she sobbed, shudders of anguish and torment shaking her frame as she gave way to tears of overwhelming grief and desolation.

'Leonie! You don't understand! You are so terribly wrong—it is not like that at all.' A deep groan broke from his throat as he seized her tightly in his arms, kissing her with rough, mounting passion.

Appalled, Leonie realised that her treacherous body was responding to his firm embrace and inflaming lips. With an almighty effort she managed to push him away, far enough to allow her to slip from beneath his arms and roll across the bed, taking to her heels and dashing for the bathroom. Slamming the door and locking it quickly behind her, she staggered over to sit down on a stool, panting breathlessly as she ignored his angry demands that she come out and listen to what he had to say.

'Do not be foolish,' he added in a softer tone. 'You cannot stay in there forever, and I will be waiting out here—even if it takes a week. So, be sensible, hmm?'

'Go to hell!' she shouted, trying to control her limbs which seemed to be jerking as if she had St Vitus's dance. It was some time before she could even attempt to pull herself together. Sitting huddled on the stool with arms clasped tightly about her shivering body, she was only able to rock herself backwards and forwards in mindless agony. The shock of being so swiftly and abruptly transported from heaven to hell—all in a few short days—was more than she could cope with.

Eventually, her shuddering figure became still, and she tried to think what she was going to do next.

Could she make Badyr divorce her? Would he let her leave the country? She could hardly bring herself to face the fact, but it seemed certain that he would refuse to do either of those things. So, what could she do? She was alone in the country, with no real friends and no help at hand. Badyr was absolute ruler of Dhoman, and what he said was, *ipso facto*, the law. There was no one who would raise a hand to assist her, not when they knew they would inevitably incur his wrath. And yet, to submit to him, to have him make love to her—straight from another woman's bed, as Nadia had so succinctly put it—was so intolerable that . . . Never! she promised herself, gasping with pain. She must never let him possess her again! But how was she to stop him? She knew very well that fight him as she might, his superior strength would always prevail in the end. And even if her body didn't betray her, as she very much feared that it would, his need for sons to follow him on the throne was such that he wouldn't hesitate to rape her if necessary. The baby! Could she possibly use the baby in any way . . .?

Totally exhausted by her storm of tears, she moved over to the shower on legs which felt as if they would collapse any moment. Standing beneath the cool spray, letting the water flow over her hair and body, she gradually found that she was able to begin thinking more constructively. By the time she had dried herself, and wrapped her wet hair in a small white towel, she had managed to formulate a course of action. Although, whether it would be successful or not, she had no idea.

'Ah, I see that you have decided to be sensible,' Badyr murmured, leaning against the open window that led to the balcony. 'I have locked the door of this room, and we will stay here until you give me an opportunity to tell you exactly why I married Aisha, yes?'

'No.' Leonie said firmly, walking across the room to sit down in an easy chair. 'Why should I have to listen to your puerile excuses? I'm not in the slightest bit interested in your relationship with your other so-called wife, whom I will always regard as nothing more than your mistress. Frankly, I have far more important things on my mind than trying to keep up with your sex-life!'

'You stupid girl!' he shouted, throwing his hands in the air in exasperation.

'You are so right! Stupid is exactly what I was, but I've now decided to get smart. So—you, *my dear Badyr*,' she added caustically, through teeth which chattered loudly in her head, 'had better just shut up—and listen to me for once.'

'I will not divorce you. I will not let you go back to England—and that is my final word,' he retorted in a hard, flat voice.

'I've already realised that,' she informed him bleakly, noting a look of uncertainty flit across his face. Taking a deep breath, and trying to control her nervously shaking body, she began to lay down her terms.

'We have been married—if you can call it a marriage!—for six years. We have a little daughter and now I am expecting another child. My mother had always said that Jade needed a father, and the same must apply to the new baby. I am, therefore, prepared to stay with you, to act as your wife and to submit to your possession as best I can,' she shuddered.

'However, you have admitted that you have used me shamefully—as indeed you have! And it is only right that you should make some effort to repair the damage you have caused myself and my daughter. I must insist that you immediately divorce your second wife, Aisha. I've nothing against the woman—if anything I feel damn sorry for anyone involved with you—but my children need the sole attention of their father. To put it bluntly: I'm not prepared to have Jade's view of life corrupted by the sight of her father's flagrant immorality!' She paused. 'Have I made myself quite clear?' she demanded harshly.

'Yes, Leonie. Very clear,' Badyr retorted bitterly, before turning to look out of the window, his tall figure silhouetted against the dying sun. It was a long time before he gave a deep, heavy sigh and slowly turned back to face her once again.

'You are a fool if you do not realise that I would do anything I possibly could to please you,' he said softly. 'But in this case...' He wearily shook his head. 'I cannot ... I cannot do what you ask, my darling. It would be too unkind, too cruel for my Aisha to bear.'

'*Your Aisha?* To hell with your Aisha! What about *our* daughter, and the new baby?' She took a deep breath. 'I don't care about myself, Badyr, I really don't,' she assured him earnestly. 'But what sort of life is it going to be for my children? Surely they deserve more than half a father's love. Do you really want them to grow up in the sort of life and atmosphere that you did? How can you have so quickly forgotten that terrible old palace?'

'I cannot do it, Leonie! You may be right in what you say, but I cannot do it, my darling. If you'd just let me explain ...'

'Okay—that's it!' she snapped grimly. 'I had to try and rescue something from the shambles of our marriage—if only for Jade and the baby's sake— although God knows, the thought of having to live another day with you makes me feel sick! However, it now seems that I have no choice but to give you my final ultimatum.'

'What on earth are you talking about, Leonie? If you'd just ...'

'I'm just going to tell you how it will be from now on,' she said, her voice low and deadly. 'There is, you will agree, a fifty-fifty chance that the baby I'm expecting is the son you want so much?'

'Yes, of course, but . . .'

'Right, let's see how badly you want that child, Badyr. You are going to leave this palace tonight—together with the rest of your family—leaving me, Jade, Miss Jackson, Hussa and sufficient servants to make sure we are all comfortable.'

'No!' he retorted furiously.

'Oh yes—this is where I am going to live—without you, I'm happy to say! I am quite prepared to send Jade to see you once a month, but you will never—*never*—so much as set foot in this palace, ever again.'

'And what makes you think that I will agree to such a preposterous idea?' he demanded angrily.

'Are you a betting man? How do the odds of two-to-one attract you? If you leave me here, I will give you your son—maybe. However, if you make me live with you, forcing your revolting attentions upon me, I will deliberately abort the baby I'm expecting and any others that I might conceive.'

'I don't believe you!' he snarled, his face as white as chalk. 'It would be a sin to do such a thing.'

Leonie shrugged as carelessly as she could. She had to try and make Badyr too angry to think clearly, and to be as convincing as possible if she hoped to get away with her bluff.

'What is sin? As far as I'm concerned it would be a far worse crime to bring a new baby into our present lives. To have our son grow up realising that his father is a bigamist!'

'Don't you dare use that word!' he bellowed with rage.

'The facts speak for themselves,' she snapped. 'However, let's keep to the point. Unless you are prepared to lock me up in one of your father's dungeons, I can assure you that I will terminate this pregnancy. And there isn't a damn thing you can do about it!' She saw that he was hesitating, and quickly pressed home her advantage before she lost her nerve in saying the terrible words.

'Of course, you might be like your dreadful old father—maybe you'd get a *real* thrill out of having me chained to a dank prison wall for the next eight months? It would make the time dear old Sultan Raschid had you confined here, in this palace, seem like a picnic—wouldn't it?' she murmured, encouraged by his hard, bleak expression to go for the *coup de grâce*. 'Ah well, you had better unlock the door and call the guards in to arrest me.'

'My God, you're a clever woman—just like my mother!' he whispered with cold rage. 'That is a very dramatic performance you have just given—you know damn well that any question of prison is ridiculous! What is more, I don't believe for one moment that you would harm our unborn child, but you know I cannot take the risk that you might do so.'

He swore violently under his breath as he paced up and down before the windows, clearly trying to find a way out of Leonie's ultimatum. 'Very well, Leonie,' Badyr said at last, his voice cold as ice as he turned to face her. 'You win—it shall be as you say.'

Despite her total misery and her loathing of the man who had so destroyed her life, she felt a sudden pang as she looked at his bowed shoulders and the lines of strain on his face as he went over to open the door.

'Oh Badyr,' she sighed wearily. 'Can't you see? Can't you understand—that once you deserted me and married another woman, you set in train this . . . this ghastly, unhappy mess in which we find ourselves? You talk about winning,' she gave another deep, heavy sigh, 'there are no winners in this affair—only losers, I'm afraid.'

He turned, pausing to look at her for some moments, his face a blank mask. 'I am not a loser, Leonie. And you would do well to remember that fact in the future!'

His cold, harsh warning seemed to permeate the still air of the room long after he had slammed the door behind him.

CHAPTER EIGHT

HUSSA showed the doctor out of the bedroom, leaving
Leonie to dress herself in privacy. Checking her make-
up in the mirror, she grimaced at the reflection of her
heavy figure before walking slowly and carefully down
the stairs to the main room of the palace.

'Would you like a cool drink before you go?' she
asked Dr Winslow, the brilliant young American
gynaecologist at the new hospital in Muria, who had
been assigned by Badyr to monitor her pregnancy.

'I'd love one,' he grinned. 'I never need any excuse to
delay leaving this lovely part of the country. It sure is a
great place!'

'Yes, I'm very happy here, it's so peaceful and quiet,'
she said, ringing for a servant and ordering some fresh
lime juice.

'Well, I guess you'd better make the most of it. I
reckon this is likely to be my last visit before the
monsoon sets in, and I gather that there is no way you
are going to be able to stay down here in the south
when that happens. Besides,' he added, 'you're seven
months pregnant now and I'll need to give you more
than the monthly check we've been having so far.'

'Oh, no!' Leonie checked her outburst as the servant
returned with the cool drinks. 'I'm really very well, and
what is a little rain to someone who is used to English
weather?' She gave him a soft, cajoling smile. 'Couldn't
you persuade my husband to let me stay down here for
another month, at least?'

He looked at the lovely girl and regretfully shook his
head. 'I sure am sorry,' he said, 'and I truly understand
why you don't want to leave. But I just can't do it. I
had enough trouble persuading your husband not to

haul you back to Muria last month—he'll never go for it again, I'm afraid.'

'But I'm perfectly fit and well.'

'Hmm. Yes, in general I'd agree. But your blood pressure is up a little, and with under two months to go.' He paused and shook his head. 'If it wasn't for the monsoon, I might possibly have been able to swing it— to allow you to stay here for a while. However, what with the bad weather coming soon and the need for more frequent medical checks, I'd have to agree with the Sultan. I'm sorry, but . . .' He shrugged his shoulders.

Gazing at the beautiful girl's unhappy expression, he wished that he didn't have to be the bearer of what she clearly regarded as bad news. There was obviously trouble between the Sultan and his wife, and it was a shame to see two people tearing each other apart; although after a shaky start to her pregnancy it now looked as if the wife was in better shape than the husband. Still, the Sultan had his own doctors, and it was up to them to tell him to take it easy. He could only be glad that it wasn't his job to try and talk some sense into that austere, taciturn figure. Sultan Badyr, once such a likable and approachable guy, had lately become so hard, tough and bad-tempered, that it would take a brave man to tell him that if he didn't slow down on his work-load, sooner or later he was going to be seriously ill.

Leonie sighed. 'Well, as you said, I'll just have to make the most of the time I've got left,' she murmured, realising that it was unfair on the doctor to protest any more. By getting the last two months' extension he'd already done as much as he could for her, and to push him any further was unreasonable.

Walking slowly through the garden, Leonie sank down on to a bench beneath a wide, shady palm-tree. It was almost six months since she had been left alone in this palace, desperately unhappy and heart-stricken at the discovery of Badyr's second wife. As the weeks had passed slowly by, the peace and calm of the quiet life had provided some measure of balm for her troubled spirits, but nothing it seemed could banish her love for Badyr, or the wretched misery at the choice he had made.

She hadn't—she didn't—wanted to know anything about his other wife, Aisha. But that didn't stop the evil, insidious jealousy from winding its slimy green tentacles around her heart. Night after night she hadn't been able to stop torturing herself with the thought of Badyr making love to another woman—a woman that he had refused to relinquish, and who therefore meant far more to him than Leonie had ever done.

Those first few months, living day and night with the haunting vision of Badyr's long, tanned body lying closely entwined with another woman, his erotic lovemaking arousing and inflaming another woman's passion, had led to a serious decline in her health. Growing daily more thin and strained, her face gaunt and pale with dark shadows beneath her dull blue eyes, she had only been jerked from the dark depths of her misery and depression by Dr Winslow's hard words.

'Look here,' he had said. 'The Sultan has made me entirely responsible for your health during this pregnancy. The baby is fine at the moment, but I can't say the same goes for you! After my last trip, I had to tell your husband that I wasn't happy about you—it would have been worth more than my life not to—and he hit the roof!' He looked at the haggardly beautiful girl with compassion.

'So, okay, I'm not blind and anyone can see you've got problems, but you've got to try and pull yourself together. I'll do what I can for you, but you're going to have to co-operate and make a big effort. Otherwise, I can promise you that the Sultan will override anything I say, and insist that you go back to Muria. You may be able to stop him doing that, but I sure as hell can't!'

The threat that she might be forced to return to Badyr had been enough to help pull her at least halfway out of her depressed state, and the slow march of time had done the rest. She was still bitterly unhappy, but she had made a determined effort to banish from her mind the sensual images of Badyr's lean, hard figure, and to control the overwhelming sexual jealousy, which had been so tormenting her days and nights. She wasn't always successful, of course, but very gradually she had begun to put on some more weight, the colour coming back to her cheeks and the life to her sapphire-blue eyes.

'Attagirl!' Dr Winslow had said on his next monthly visit, looking at her glowing beauty with appreciative eyes. 'Just keep on the way you're going, and you'll be fine.'

A shout in the distance interrupted her thoughts, and she looked up to see Jade racing over the grass towards her.

'I caught a fish—I did, really!' Jade danced with excitement. 'But Miss Jackson said it was only a baby fish, and so I had to put it back.'

'You'll be able to catch it again next year, and it will be much bigger then, just like you!' Elizabeth laughed as she joined them, carrying the fishing rod which was Jade's latest present from her great-uncle Feisal.

'Can we go fishing tomorrow?' Jade demanded. 'Maybe Mummy can come too—oh, please do say that you will, Mummy?' she added, giving Leonie a hug and laughing as she felt the baby moving in her mother's womb. 'I bet the baby would like to go fishing. I do wish it would hurry up and arrive, 'cos I want to show it my collection of shells.'

'Well, you'll have to wait just a little bit longer,' Leonie said as she stood up, and taking Jade's hand began to walk slowly back to the palace. 'Although I think it might be some time before the new baby will be able to appreciate your collection, I'm afraid!'

'Did the doctor give you a clean bill of health?'
Elizabeth asked as they stopped to allow Jade to pick
some flowers.

'Yes, I'm fine. But it looks as if we'll have to leave
here fairly soon. Apparently the monsoon is due to hit
this area of the country very shortly, and when that
happens, we must return to Muria.'

'Never mind. It's been an idyll—as far as I'm
concerned, anyway. And although you may not want to
return, you're going to be so busy getting all the
necessary bits and pieces ready for the baby, that you
really won't have time to think of much else.'

Leonie smiled gratefully at Elizabeth. Looking back,
it seemed incredible that she had once been annoyed
with Badyr for engaging the governess. Elizabeth had
been such a quiet tower of strength during these last
months, that she didn't know what she would have
done without her.

Not that Leonie had confided in the other girl, of
course. But she imagined that Elizabeth must have a
very good idea of exactly why the Sultan and his wife
were so estranged. The governess had been here with
Jade at the Summer Palace when the whole terrible
business—Nadia's revelation about Badyr's second
wife—had blown up in Leonie's face, and there couldn't
have been many there who didn't know the reason why
Badyr had so suddenly ordered everyone out of the
place. Any remaining doubts would have been removed
by the subsequent, monumental row between Nadia
and Badyr.

Leonie had resolutely refused to leave her bedroom,
but even from there she could hear Badyr's thunderous
roars of anger as he vented his rage over the head of the
hapless girl. When Sara had come in to kiss Leonie
farewell, she had been shivering and shaking from the
scene downstairs.

'I warned her,' Sara had muttered through teeth that
were still chattering with nervous tension. 'But, *wallahi!*,

I did not realise just how bad it would be. My brother is as one demented! Oh, Leonie, I am so desperately sorry and unhappy for you.'

'Don't let's talk about it, please,' Leonie had whispered, very near to breaking down again. 'I—I can't face any more discussion of the subject, I really can't.'

'But, surely Badyr explained . . .'

'Oh, yes, he explained all right!' she had grated, before the events of the day proved too much for her and she ran into the bathroom to be violently sick. Sara hadn't wanted to leave her at that point, but Leonie had insisted. Sweet though the girl was, she simply didn't feel she could take any more of Badyr's family. She hadn't of course set eyes on Sara since, and as to what had happened to Nadia, she had no idea.

'Well, Jade and I had better start packing and getting all our things together,' Elizabeth said calmly. 'Little madam, over there, will be overjoyed to return to Muria—and her pony!' She looked over to where Jade had wandered off after some flowers across the glade. 'I haven't said much to you, since there's been no point in making a meal out of the situation, but there's no doubt that Jade has been missing her father a great deal, and finding the monthly visits very confusing, I'm afraid.'

'I know,' Leonie sighed. 'But there hasn't been anything I could do about it—not really.'

'Never mind. She'll soon perk up and settle down when we get back. Children are very resilient, you know,' Elizabeth murmured sympathetically. 'And with her pony and her stu-pen-dous uncle Feisal, she'll soon forget all her worries!'

'Oh, Elizabeth,' Leonie gave a shaky laugh. 'You're a terrible governess! Surely you could have taught her another favourite word by now?'

'Hmm, I have tried, but none of the ones I suggest seem to have taken root in that active little brain. The main trouble is that the interesting sounding words are, more often than not, thoroughly rude—if not downright pornographic!'

'What's por-no-graph-ic mean, Mummy?' Jade asked, having come up without the two women hearing her approach. 'Why are you and Miss Jackson laughing like that? Shall I take these flowers in to Hussa, I'm sure she will like them.'

'I'm sure she will, darling,' Leonie laughed and took her hand. 'Come on, it is nearly time for lunch, and I'm sure you must be hungry,' she added as they walked back into the house.

The young doctor's warning had proved to be correct, Leonie realised, when Sheikh Samir flew down to see her three days later.

'His Majesty suggests that you might consider being ready to leave in four days' time. The meteorological report is not good, and he is anxious that you should be well away from this area before the rains come.'

'I think that is more of an order than a suggestion, don't you?' Leonie murmured wryly. 'However, you may tell the Sultan that I shall concur with his wishes. Where . . . er . . . where exactly are my daughter and I going to live?'

The young sheikh looked at her in surprise. 'You will be taken to your home, of course. To the palace in Muria.'

'I see.'

'However, his Majesty has asked me to tell you that . . . er . . . most unfortunately he will be unable to . . . er . . . welcome you back to Muria in person. It is a matter that I am sure he . . . er . . . very much regrets.' The Sheikh cleared his throat nervously. 'However, I understand that he is about to undertake a tour of the country, and is likely to be away for the next six weeks. He has asked me to assure you that he will, of course, return in ample time to be with you on the birth of his child.'

Leonie sat back in her chair. 'You know, Sheikh, I

really do feel that you are wasted in your present job. The diplomacy with which you so charmingly translate your master's commands and edicts has my complete and utter admiration. You should surely be an ambassador, at the very least!'

Sheikh Samir flinched at the caustic tone in Leonie's dry voice. 'I merely try to convey his Majesty's ... er ...'

'I know,' she said quickly, instantly contrite for taking out her unhappiness and frustration on the young man, who was having to carry out Badyr's orders. 'I must apologise for my bad manners, and I hope you will forgive me for being so tiresome.'

'Of course, Majesty,' he smiled. 'I realise it is not an easy time for you—with the baby's birth imminent, I mean,' he added hastily. 'And I can assure you, with total sincerity, that it has been a very great pleasure to have been able to visit you over these last few months.'

'Oh, Sheikh Samir!' she laughed softly. 'You really *are* a splendid diplomat! Now, do please relax. Tell me—how is Maryam?'

'The Princess Maryam is very well,' he assured her, going on to describe a picnic organised by her Prince Feisal at which, Leonie gathered, the Sheikh and Maryam had been able to spend some time together.

Leonie no longer wondered why Maryam had been so awkward in her company, when she had returned to Dhoman. She now saw that Badyr's sister had known all about his second wife, and due to the friendship between them in the past, had found the necessity of suppressing that knowledge more difficult than the other members of the royal family.

'Do please give Maryam my love,' she said as the young ADC prepared to leave. 'And tell her that I do understand, and despite all that has passed, I hope she will feel she can come and see me when I return to Muria.'

The Sheikh, to his eternal credit, didn't pretend not

to know what Leonie was talking about, but merely
bowed over her hand as he promised to deliver the
message.

Leonie was deeply unhappy to leave, but even she was
forced to see the sense behind their hasty departure
when the heavens opened a day before they left. The
thick fog and the never-ending, heavy sheet of
pounding rain was as depressing as Badyr had said it
would be, and Leonie regretfully resigned herself to her
fate. She found some measure of cheer in reflecting that
the weather would clear in three months' time, when
she would be able to return to the peace and seclusion
of the summer palace.

Maybe because she was heavily pregnant it seemed a
long, hard journey back to the capital city. By the time
she arrived at the palace, Leonie's ankles were puffy
and swollen and she felt weary and exhausted. Wearing
long filmy robes, the traditional dress of Dhomani
women, wasn't just sensible in the heat but might have
been specifically designed to hide the bulky figures of
pregnant women, she thought wryly as she lay soaking
in the bath.

Of course, part of the reason she felt so exhausted
must be due to the nervous strain of having to return to
this place. She had spoken caustically to Sheikh Samir
about his polite explanation of Badyr's planned
absence, but she really ought to be thankful that her
husband had chosen to go away. Having to live cheek
by jowl with him in an atmosphere of ever-present
enmity would have been more than she could bear. And
what was Badyr planning to do when she had given
birth to the baby? Her threats to harm her unborn
child—something she could *never* have brought herself
to actually carry out—would be useless. However,
maybe if she had a boy—a son to follow him on the
throne—he would feel no need of further procreation?
She fervently hoped so.

A noise in the next room broke through her thoughts. It must be Hussa with the light supper she had ordered, Leonie realised, and removed the bath plug before trying to get out of the large, sunken bath. Unfortunately, it was of a different design from the one she had been used to in the summer palace.

'Please come and give me a hand, Hussa,' she called out. 'I think I've got stuck in the bath!' she added with a laugh.

Hearing footsteps approaching, she turned to smile at Hussa and nearly fainted when she saw not her old servant ... but the tall figure of Badyr! Her eyes widened in fear, her body trembling as she saw him pause inside the door for a moment before putting out a hand to collect a large fluffy towel, and walking slowly over the marble floor to where she lay trapped in the bath.

'W-what are you doing here?' she gasped. 'I ... I thought you had g-gone away.' The blood drummed through her veins as she viewed his tall figure, her dazed eyes noticing that he had discarded his black patch and his usual traditional dress, his broad-shouldered frame clothed only in a short towelling robe.

'Unfortunately, I have had no choice but to delay my journey,' he retorted curtly. 'I can assure you that it is not on *your* account, my dear Leonie, that I am still in Muria,' he added in a cold, hard voice. 'God knows I do not ...'

Badyr drew in a sharp breath, his eyes darkening as he stared down at her body, completely revealed as the last of the bath-water gurgled away. Instinctively, she folded her arms, trying to shield the heavy swell of her stomach and the full ripeness of her breasts.

'No! Let me look at you.' He knelt down to grasp her hands, moving them aside as his eyes travelled down the length of her body. 'My child—my son,' he breathed thickly. She flinched as he reached for her, but his

touch was surprisingly gentle as he lifted her out o
the bath and enfolded her shaking figure in the sof
towel.

'How could I have forgotten your gloriously sof
flesh?' he murmured, drying her arms and shoulder
before moving gently down to the burgeoning swell o
her breasts. 'So pale . . . so soft and smooth, like silke
velvet.'

'Please, no!' Her low moan of protest was ignored a
his hands took the place of the towel, moving erotically
over the rosy peaks that hardened and throbbed at hi
touch.

'Let me go!' she cried, struggling in vain as he quickl
tossed aside the towel, adroitly capturing her wrists and
holding them in one of his broad hands behind he
back. Arching her body towards him, he allowed hi
other hand to move tenderly and carefully over the tau
mound of her enlarged womb, her body quivering and
trembling at his touch and the intensity of his gaze a
his eyes devoured the sight of her changed contours.

His action and her nervous response provoked a
reaction as she felt the baby give a protesting kick
Badyr looked at her with startled eyes, his face pale and
tense as he quickly released her.

'Your son—or daughter—is clearly feeling energeti
tonight,' she muttered, her teeth chattering nervously a
she grabbed the towel; she was still feeling stunned b
his unexpected appearance, her senses bemused by th
heavy atmosphere of sexual tension which crackled lik
electricity between them.

'That is really . . .? You mean . . .?' He stared i
fascination at her stomach as her trembling hand
fought with the towel, clumsily trying to hide he
nakedness from his sight.

'Oh, Badyr! Surely you know how babies kick?'

'No—how should I? I was not present when yo
were expecting Jade,' he retorted savagely. 'And i
would seem, would it not, that once again I have bee

denied the pleasure of seeing my child grow in your womb?'

Leonie was confused by the harsh, bitter tone in his voice. Looking at him more closely, she was disturbed to see the deep lines of strain on his face, and surely . . . surely he used not to have silver threads among the black hair at his temples? To her utter consternation, she was suddenly swept by an overwhelming and extraordinary urge to comfort the man gazing at her with such bleak intensity. Without conscious thought Leonie moved slowly towards him, pulling aside the towel as she took his hand and placed it on her stomach.

'You see?' she whispered as the child within her moved again. 'Sometimes babies aren't very active, but as you can see this one—so like its father!—kicks very hard indeed.'

Although he gave a grunt of laughter at her words, there was a strange look of awe on his tanned face. 'It seems a miracle that my child should be growing in such a way, and that he will soon be born into this world,' he murmured. 'But come, Leonie,' he added a few moments later, gently lifting her up in his arms. 'I was told that you arrived very tired and exhausted, so you must now rest.'

'No, please, please put me down, Badyr. I have to oil my body, and really I'm feeling much . . . much . . .' She couldn't continue, a hard lump in her throat preventing her from saying any more. She could feel his hard chest muscles and the warmth of his skin through the thin towelling, the harsh planes of his tanned cheek so close to her own and the familiar scent of his cologne filling her nostrils. It was all so evocative of their deliriously happy moments together in the past, those deeply sensual, intimate hours they had spent making love to one another, that she seemed incapable of protest as she felt all her willpower draining away.

Reminding herself of his despicable conduct appeared

to have no effect on the languorous, drowsy lassitude which was seeping through her mind and body as he carried her through into the bedroom. Laying her carefully and tenderly down on the bed, he left her to return a few moments later with a bottle in his hands.

'There is no need to worry, my Leonie,' he murmured, sitting down on the bed beside her. 'I will smooth the oil on for you.'

'Oh, no, you mustn't . . . it's quite wrong, and I'm so ugly like this.'

'On the contrary,' he breathed huskily, ignoring her weakly fluttering hands as he parted the towel to reveal her naked body. 'I have never seen you looking so lovely—or so very, very desirable.'

Pouring some of the liquid into his palm, he began to massage the taut skin of her stomach, moving his hands slowly and gently over her flesh. 'How can you think that I would not wish to see your body, especially when it is ripe and swollen with my child?' he murmured, rhythmically smoothing the oil over her skin.

There seemed to be a humming noise in her ears as a lambent warmth coursed through her body. She sighed deeply, incapable of any effort of will or desire to stop his caressing fingers, mindlessly responding to their sensual touch. Cupping her full, ripe breasts in his hands, he lowered his dark head to brush his lips tantalisingly over her taut nipples, Leonie moaning aloud at the thrilling ache deep in her stomach.

'You see?' he breathed. 'We are the two halves of one whole. Hate and loathe me as you will, my beloved, but you cannot deny the innate need and desire we have for each other.'

He was right. However much she wanted to protest and refute his hoarsely whispered words, Leonie realised that she was helpless beneath the erotic mastery of his hands; a soft yet demanding arousal that provoked a quivering, heated response in her traitorous body.

'Badyr . . . no!' she moaned as he put aside the lotion and swiftly removed his towelling robe.

'Oh, my Leonie . . . *yes!*' he muttered thickly, his face a tight mask of desire, the dark eyes glittering with mockery at the lack of conviction in her voice.

The arms that enfolded her trembling body were hard and warm, his mouth descending to kiss away the hopeless tears which had filled her eyes, before trailing down her cheek to seek the soft hollows at the base of her throat. There was a raw hunger in the hands and lips caressing her soft flesh, a devouring, demanding need that met an answering response. It was as if she was in the grip of a hallucinatory drug, every one of her senses, every nerve-end, screamingly aware of his breath on her skin, the heavy pounding beat of his heart and the black silky hair on his chest brushing against the tips of her breasts. Her body shook with an overwhelming desire that she could not possibly deny, her hands feathering down the long length of his spine and moving over the taut, firm muscles of his hips and thighs.

A deep groan was wrenched from his throat at her intimate, caressing touch, his figure shaking as he possessed her lips with an urgency that finally swept aside all the barriers between them. Leonie clung blindly to his broad shoulders, totally abandoning herself to the ardour that flared through her body and murmuring soft, incoherent cries of delight as his lips and hands moved over her flesh with scorching intensity; burning and demanding her total surrender.

'My sweet Leonie . . . it has been such a long time . . . such torture! For God's sake do not deny me, my darling!' he whispered thickly, the words rasping in his throat, his chest heaving as though it pained him to breathe. 'I will be gentle and careful, but I cannot resist your lovely body. I must . . . *I must have you!*'

Neither the moral values of right and wrong, nor the unhappy past nor the uncertain future seemed to have

any meaning for Leonie as she feverishly responded to
the overwhelming desire which held them both firmly in
its thrall. Here and now, the only reality was the hard
warmth and strength of his tanned body, and the
almost unbearable ecstasy that raced through her veins.
Almost unconscious with delirious excitement, she
barely heard the low, deep groans provoked by the
wanton abandonment of her response; her soft moans
and pleas for fulfilment an irresistible enticement,
provoking heated shudders that shook the tanned
length of his long body as he strove to maintain his self-
control.

As he had promised, Badyr managed to temper the
urgency of his desire, leashing and controlling the force
of his own passion as he gently and tenderly led her
from one exquisite delight to another; the mounting
pleasure so prolonged and emotionally intense that she
cried out, weeping with joy as he at last brought them
both to a soaring high plateau of mutual ecstasy and
overwhelming rapture. Thereafter, floating on a hazy
cloud of warmth and happiness, Leonie drifted
aimlessly down into a deep sleep, aware only of the
comfort and security as she lay within Badyr's
encircling arms.

The sun was pouring into the bedroom when Leonie
woke next morning, and she drowsily stretched her
languid, satiated body before slowly turning her head to
see that she was alone in the middle of the great bed.
Her eyes widened with horror and disbelief as she noted
the crumpled sheets, the pillow still bearing the imprint
of Badyr's head. Inexorably and relentlessly the events
of the previous night flashed through her mind like a
reel of film out of control, and with a deep groan of
despair she rolled over to bury her head in the pillows.

Oh God! How ... how could she? How could she
possibly have allowed herself to submit to him? And it
was worse than that! *Far, far worse!* She hadn't just
weakly given in to his amorous demands, had she?

Leonie moaned with self-loathing and disgust as she remembered exactly how she had responded, how eagerly and lasciviously she had demanded his possession.

Shivering and shaking she turned over, seeking a handkerchief to staunch the tears of bitter remorse which were flooding down her cheeks. A sound attracted her attention and she glanced sideways to see the swirling white robes of Badyr's tall figure as he entered the room.

'*No!* Go away!' she cried hysterically. 'Oh God! How I wish I'd never b-been b-b-born!'

Not able to control the sobs that shuddered through her trembling body, she hung her head, tears blinding her vision as she stared fixedly down at her fingers clutching the sheet in wild agitation.

There was a long silence as Badyr came to a halt beside the bed, staring down at the girl who was weeping so bitterly. His lips tightened into a hard line as he viewed the disordered cloud of her magnificent red-gold hair, her figure shaking as if in the grip of some tropical fever.

'I realise that it is no excuse to say that I could not prevent myself from behaving as I did last night,' he grated harshly. 'The sweet enticement of your body would tempt even a saint—and God knows I am but a frail, mortal man.' He paused for a moment as she buried her face in her hands, shaken by a fresh paroxysm of convulsive sobs.

'Unfortunately, as much as I would wish to do so, there is a very good, pressing reason why I cannot leave Muria at the moment. However, I am not prepared to allow scandal or gossip to touch my house and family,' he declared in a cold, hard voice. 'I must, therefore, continue to use this palace as I have always done, until such time as I can depart on my tour of the country. Nevertheless, my dear Leonie,' he added with savage bitterness, 'you have no need to worry. I can give you my complete assurance that you will be quite safe from what you clearly regard as my vile attentions. I trust I make myself clear?'

Exhausted by her storm of weeping and stunned by the harsh ferocity of his voice, Leonie could do no more than nod her head, waiting with quivering, nervous tension to hear what else he had to say. However, the heavy silence was only broken by the swishing sound of his long, white robes as Badyr spun abruptly on his heel and swiftly left the room.

CHAPTER NINE

TOWARDS the end of what seemed to have been the longest three weeks of her life, Leonie was quite sure she had never before been quite so miserably unhappy, despite all that had happened in the past. It was as though she inhabited a desperately lonely, wretched state of purgatory, where nothing could lift the heavy weight of her despair.

Tension headaches plagued her during the succeeding long hot days, giving her no rest from the terrible realisation that she was trapped: both by the imminent birth of her baby, and a daughter whom she could not possibly abandon, but also by the knowledge of how desperately she yearned for Badyr's arms; a longing which haunted her every conscious moment. He was her first thought on waking and her last at night. His presence even haunted her disturbed, restless sleep as his tall, charismatic figure strode relentlessly through her dreams. His cruel abandonment, his callous disregard and total insensitivity was an ever-present torture—a terminal illness from which it seemed she would never recover.

If only she had not asked old Sultan Raschid for tuition in Arabic, all those years ago. Maybe, if she hadn't been able to speak the language, she might have been spared the knowledge of exactly where and with whom Badyr was spending his days. Unfortunately, she had inadvertently overheard a conversation between two of the palace servants. From what they said, it had been abundantly clear that the Sultan was in constant attendance on his second wife, Aisha, at her palace up in the hills behind Muria.

Despite the painful knowledge of her husband's

scandalous, almost obscene behaviour, it seemed that
nothing could destroy the deep feelings she had for him.
If, as she did, she constantly told herself how much she
hated Badyr, she was also full of bitter self-loathing for
her own emotional weakness. She couldn't even accuse
him of not keeping his word, given the last time they
had spoken to each other. She was always fast asleep
when he joined her in the large bed, and had left it long
before she opened her eyes in the morning—only the
lingering aroma of his distinctive cologne betraying the
fact that he spent his nights lying beside her.

Maryam had called one afternoon, the brief visit
proving to be a heavy strain on them both. Leonie,
whose head was pounding with a migraine, felt quite
unable to talk about her desperate situation, while
Maryam had been clearly shocked and horrified by the
sight of the English girl's haggard beauty, the bleak
misery in her sapphire-blue eyes. Keeping their
conversation to such innocuous topics as Jade's
enthusiasm for her pony and her scholastic progress
under the supervision of Elizabeth Jackson, Maryam
did let fall the information that a few days previously
Sara had given birth to a little girl.

'Uncle Hassan is delighted with his new daughter,'
Maryam enthused, before blushing fiercely at her *faux
pas*. Mention of her uncle and his new child could only
lead to the dangerous topic of his eldest daughter,
Aisha. 'I . . . er . . . I went to visit Sara yesterday. She's
in the new Maternity Hospital,' she continued quickly.
'It is really a wonderful place, Leonie, and all the
nurses—who are British and American—seem to be so
friendly. Are you having your baby there?'

Leonie shrugged her shoulders. 'Yes, I think so,' she
muttered, realising with a pang that she should have
given more thought to the necessary details and
arrangements for the birth of her child. 'I'm so pleased
that Sara has the little girl she wanted, please give her my
love,' she added, feeling ashamed of the envy she felt

for Sara who, unlike herself, had the loving warmth and
support of her husband at such a time.

The tense, strained atmosphere between them had
caused Maryam to cut her visit short, and when the
arrival of Sultana Zenobia was announced a few days
later, Leonie asked Hussa to make her apologies. The
thought of having to go through the trauma of yet
another round of polite conversation was more than she
felt she could cope with.

'Stuff and nonsense! I have no intention of going
away without seeing her Majesty,' the older woman
stated firmly, brushing the servant aside as she strode
regally into Leonie's private sitting-room. Taking no
notice of her daughter-in-law's obvious reluctance to
see her, she proceeded to sit down in a comfortable
chair, giving Leonie a searching glance from beneath
her heavy eye-lids.

'Hmm. I can see that Maryam was quite right. It is
plainly obvious that matters between you and my son
have reached a desperate state.'

'I . . . er . . . I really don't want to discuss . . .'

'How long is it before the birth of your child?'
Zenobia asked, as Leonie slowly raised her ungainly
body from the *chaise-longue* on which she had been
lying, and rang the bell for a servant to bring in the
coffee which was traditionally served to visitors on their
arrival.

'About a month,' she muttered, returning to lie back
against the soft cushions.

'One would have thought Badyr could see how he is
endangering the birth of the son he desires so much—
the stupid man!' Zenobia shook her head, clicking her
tongue in exasperation. 'Very well,' she added firmly, 'I
can see that despite his orders to the contrary, I clearly
have no choice but to resolve this unfortunate business
as swiftly as possible.'

Imperiously clapping her hands for Hussa, the
Sultana completely ignored Leonie's protests as she

instructed the maid to bring a shawl for her mistress, before sweeping the breathless English girl out of the palace and into a waiting limousine. Reeling under the swift turn of events, Leonie demanded to know what was going on.

'Despite being motivated by the very best of intentions, I once did you and my son a great injury. I believed that I was right at the time, but . . .' The older woman gave a weary shrug of her shoulders as the vehicle sped through the streets of Muria. 'Oh, yes, I have had years in which to realise that I was wrong—that I had, in fact, made a tragic mistake.'

Leonie looked at her in silent confusion.

'It is important that you understand how it was when you first came to this country,' the Sultana mused quietly. 'I must tell you that I was completely devastated when Badyr arrived back in Dhoman with you as his new wife. I was horrified by what my son had done—especially in view of the past history of the family. Badyr's grandfather married a French woman as his first wife,' she explained. 'And although their child was the eldest son, the ruling sheikhs of the time refused to accept the boy's mixed blood. Ignoring his just claim, they chose his younger brother, by another Arab wife, to rule Dhoman.'

'I really don't see . . .' Leonie looked at her in puzzlement.

Sultana Zenobia sighed with impatience. 'You are an intelligent girl, so surely you can understand how it was? I had schemed and planned to get Badyr out of the country, insisting that he be educated abroad, and made strenuous efforts to keep him well away from his father's increasing madness. And then—what did my son do? *He returned to Dhoman with a foreign bride!*' She sighed deeply.

'But Badyr has no other brothers.'

'I could not rely on that fact. There was no guarantee that Fatima would not have a son, or the ruling sheikhs might decide to adopt Hassan or Feisal on my husband's death—see how Hassan has married Sara, and already has a young son.' Zenobia waved her hand dismissively. 'Besides, after Badyr's arrest, my spies told me that my husband was seriously planning to disinherit his son in favour of Hassan. I had to move quickly, Leonie. It is important that you understand that I had no alternative but to make sure that you left the country—something which, Allah knows, I had tried to achieve since the day you arrived at the palace! Once you had left the country, I would then be able to marry my son off to a proper Arab wife. It would be easy to rally support behind him, once he was suitably married, and ensure that when he escaped from his prison, nothing would stand in his way. There would be no impediment to prevent him from taking over control of Dhoman from his father.'

Leonie gasped. 'You mean . . .?'

'Yes. For Badyr—for my son's life, his safety and the future good of this country—I did what I had to do.'

'So, it is *you* I have to thank for everything that has happened to me!' Leonie ground out harshly. 'My God—I hope you're pleased with your handiwork!'

'No, I have told you that I now see I was wrong. Please, please calm yourself,' she added hurriedly, putting a restraining hand on the arm of the furiously angry girl sitting beside her.

'Don't you touch me, you . . . you evil woman!' Leonie cried. 'Have you any idea of the heartbreak you've caused me? And don't keep telling me to calm down!' she added with a snarl. 'My God—there's nothing to choose between you and your son—*the spineless bastard*!'

'You do not understand.'

'You're damn right—I don't!' Leonie retorted savagely. 'It's quite clear that I've never understood my husband! How could Badyr have let himself be ordered around like that? It's almost unbelievable!' Her voice rose incredulously. 'I knew he was ambitious—but to meekly do as he was told? Tossing me aside and cheerfully marrying another woman?' She couldn't go on, almost choking with rage and fury.

'*Leonie!* Be silent and listen to me!' Zenobia ordered, catching hold of the younger girl's hands and holding them firmly in her own for a moment. 'It was not as you think. No, not at all!'

'Oh, God!' Leonie sighed heavily, slumping back in her seat and closing her eyes. 'Please take me back to the palace.'

'No—I cannot do that.'

'What?' Leonie turned her head to look at Zenobia, a frown creasing her tired brow.

The older woman hesitated for a moment. 'I am taking you to see Aisha.'

'*Oh, no!*' Leonie sat bolt upright, her eyes flashing with anger.

'Yes, yes I must. I have no choice in the matter,' Zenobia shrugged.

'Well, I certainly have! For God's sake—haven't you caused me enough trouble? Let me out of here, immediately!' she added with a sob, looking wildly about her. For the first time she noticed, through the smoked glass windows, that the car was travelling swiftly across a dusty plain towards the foothills of a far mountain range.

'Please, Leonie! I speak only the truth,' Zenobia assured her earnestly. 'I told you that I had no choice—and it is true, I haven't. Badyr's wife, Aisha . . . she is dying!'

It was some moments before Zenobia's words seeped through the chaos in Leonie's brain. 'Aisha? Dying?' She turned to stare at the older woman in bewilderment.

'Aisha made me promise—despite anything Badyr might say—that I would bring you to her. I cannot break a promise to a woman who will soon leave this life. Such a request is a solemn, binding obligation which I must obey.'

'Aisha is dying? But why? I don't understand.' Leonie shook her head in dazed confusion.

'I have been trying to tell you, but you would not listen to me,' Zenobia sighed wearily. 'To understand all, I must explain what happened when Badyr was arrested by his father and sent into exile down at the Summer Palace. Yes, I was frantic with worry for my son—what mother would not be? I knew it would only be a matter of time before my husband disinherited his son—as you know, he was growing more mad and unpredictable with each passing day. Hmm?'

'Yes, I . . .'

'However, while you remained in the palace as a hostage for Badyr's good behaviour, there was nothing I could do to gain his release. My son sent me many secret messages asking for my help to arrange your escape from Dhoman. However, I realised that he was powerless without my assistance, and so I agreed to do as he asked, but only on condition that he immediately took another wife.'

'My goodness,' Leonie's voice grated bitterly. 'What fun for Badyr!'

Zenobia winced at the girl's caustic words. 'I may well deserve your anger, but not my son, Leonie. He completely refused to agree to my terms, remaining adamantly opposed to any suggestion that he should take a second wife until he heard, from sources other than myself, of the pressure which my husband was directing against you. Only then, and because he feared for your safety—indeed, for your very life—did he most reluctantly agree to do as I wanted.'

'Are you telling me . . .?'

'I swear that what I say is the truth. As soon as I received Badyr's assent, I arranged your departure to Abu Dhabi. Badyr had no access to funds while he was imprisoned, and it was his suggestion that you be sent with some precious rugs and carpets. He said you would know how to dispose of them and have enough money on which to live, until such time as he could plan the coup against his father, divorce the wife I chose for him and bring you back to Dhoman.' Zenobia leaned back on the seat and gave a heavy sigh.

'I had no objections to my son's plans. My only desire was to see him safely on the throne and running the country—that is all.'

'And I was just a silly young girl, an expendable pawn in your game, wasn't I?' Leonie said quietly.

The Sultana shook her head. 'You were very far from being a silly young girl—how much easier my task would have been had you been so! No, Leonie, you were too young to realise it, but I saw immediately that you were too strong and independent. Despite all that I did, it was obvious that you were determined not to give in, resolved to survive all the hardships placed in your way. Not even my husband's terrible rages could manage to completely quench your spirit. Oh yes! You possessed the power to defeat all my plans—all my arrangements. I had to be rid of you before you became fully conscious of the fact.'

'*Dear God!* I really do believe you think you're paying me some sort of compliment!' Leonie lay back wearily against the seat. 'I can see it would be useless to even attempt to explain just how revolting I find your mad pursuit of power. Power, position and wealth—all gained at such a terrible cost!'

'You are right to accuse me, Leonie.' Bright patches of red stained Zenobia's cheeks. 'I accept all you say, but in my defence I must ask what you would do if your little Jade was threatened? Or the new baby, hmm? Would you not fight tooth and nail for their interests? And if you feared for their life—as I feared for my son's—can you swear to me that you would not seek to brush aside anyone or anything that stood in their way?'

There was a silence in the car as Leonie remembered how she had tried to make Badyr divorce his second wife. She hadn't cared about Aisha at that point, had she? All she had been concerned about were her children and their future welfare. Desperately wanting them to have the sole protection of their father, she had even offered to stay with Badyr, despite her full knowledge of his despicable behaviour.

She gave a heavy sigh. 'I . . . I don't know. You may be right. But I like to think that I would have been more humane. Not so terribly cruel.' She couldn't say any more as she fought to control the tears which threatened to fall any minute.

Zenobia looked at the girl sitting beside her. 'I am sorry,' she said softly. 'More sorry than you will ever realise. And it is because words of sorrow achieve nothing, that I am taking you to see Aisha today. My son will be furious. He is such a proud man, is he not? Just as proud and stubborn as you, I think!' She gave a harsh snort of wry laughter. 'I doubt that he will ever forgive me for interfering in his life, but Aisha wishes to see you. She has requested that I bring you to see her, because she has something of importance to say to you. And no, I do not know what it is that she wants to say,' she added, forestalling the question trembling on Leonie's lips. 'I am merely fulfilling the obligation she has placed on me—one that I cannot in all conscience avoid.' Zenobia hesitated. 'Come, Leonie. Will you not listen to what I have to say? Please give me a chance to explain how it was.'

'"How it was", is a phrase that seems to haunt my existence!' Leonie muttered grimly, staring blindly out of the window. 'Very well,' she said at last.

With a sigh of relief Zenobia sat back in her seat, pausing for a moment to collect her thoughts. 'After Badyr had agreed to take another wife, and with your departure from our country, it seemed as though all would go well with my arrangements. The choice of

Badyr's new bride was an obvious one. Aisha was the
daughter of my husband's brother, Hassan. I knew
that she would be approved of by my husband
especially when I pointed out to him, as I did, that
the girl would also be a hostage for Hassan's good
behaviour. Such a consideration was necessary, since
Sultan Raschid was enraged by your escape!' She
shuddered at the memory. 'However, I soon discovered that I had made a terrible mistake—not only
in seeking to interfere in my son's life, but because
knew so little about Aisha.' Zenobia gestured wearily
'Hassan had been ruling the north of the country fo
my husband, and his daughter was brought up there
I, myself, had only seen her once as a small girl and
had no idea that the tuberculosis which had killed he
mother was also already present in Aisha's lungs. She
was a pale, sickly young girl of sixteen when she wa
married by proxy and sent down to join Badyr at the
Summer Palace. There, at the height of the monsoon
she rapidly succumbed to the disease. My husband
would do nothing—although I begged him on my
knees to send a doctor down to look after the poo
child—and she gradually became more and more ill.
know that Badyr and the guards did what they could
but by the time the good weather arrived, it was too
late. The disease had gained a hold which it ha
never lost, and ever since that time, Aisha has been
very, very ill.'

'But surely tuberculosis is curable nowadays?'

Zenobia shook her head. 'Badyr has taken her to
Switzerland and seen the world's top consultants—ther
was nothing anyone could do. Eventually, she begge
him to allow her return, to let her die in peace in he
own country.'

'Oh, God—the poor girl!' Leonie looked at her i
distress. Zenobia's story, the description of Badyr'
poor sick wife in the throes of a terminal disease, was s
far removed from the glamorous 'other woman' of he

jealous fantasy, that she was hardly able to fully comprehend what she was hearing.

'And that is why my son would never divorce her. Badyr has always said that it was tragic that she should have been forced into marrying him, and that our family was totally responsible for the sharp decline in her health. He maintains that if Aisha had been left to live in the North, high in the mountain ranges, none of this would have happened to her.' Zenobia sighed. 'And yes, of course he is right, Aisha needs all his care and support for the little time she has left in this world.'

Leonie gave a low moan, hiding her face in her hands as she recalled all she had said to Badyr, the day she had discovered the existence of his other wife. 'Why did he never tell me? Why didn't he explain everything to me in London?' she whispered.

'My son does not confide in me, and there is little I can say that will be of any help to you, I'm afraid.' The older woman's voice was surprisingly warm and sympathetic. 'But I do know that Badyr was convinced you would never, never accept his second marriage— whatever the reason—and he felt he could not bring you back to Dhoman while Aisha was still alive. I can only imagine that when your mother wrote to him about her marriage, and her worries about you and Jade, that he decided to take a chance; bringing you back and hoping against hope that you would never find out about his second marriage.' She gave a wry smile. 'Men are such fools, are they not? But truly, Leonie, he has a great love for you—of that I am very certain.'

Her mind a seething mass of pain and confusion, Leonie's chaotic thoughts were interrupted as she felt the car slowing down to negotiate a series of dangerous bends through a narrow mountain pass. A few moments later they drew up outside a small white, single-storied building set on a cliff projecting out over the valley far below.

'When Aisha expressed a wish to return to Dhoman,

Badyr had this house built for her. The air up here is
purer than that down in the plain,' Zenobia murmured
as the chauffeur came around and opened the door of
the vehicle.

Trying to control her nervously trembling limbs,
Leonie found herself being helped out of the car and
following the older woman up a wide flight of steps
towards a heavy oak door. It was opened by a nurse in
a blue starched uniform, who was swiftly joined by a
young Dhomani doctor wearing a white coat.

'I'm afraid that it is only a matter of hours,' he
murmured to Zenobia, before turning to Leonie. 'You
are the Sultan's wife?'

Still feeling stunned and in a state of shock from all
that she had heard during the last hour, Leonie was
incapable of speech and only able to nod her head.

'Ah, then if you would please be so good as to come
with me,' the doctor said, taking her arm and leading
her slowly down a long corridor.

'I do beg you, Majesty, not to be alarmed by what
you see,' he murmured softly as he halted outside the
door. 'The Sultana Aisha is very weak, but I assure you
that she is in no pain. Indeed, I am hopeful that your
visit may ease her spirit, since she has been most
anxious—most determined—to speak to you. So, please
do not be distressed by her frailty and remain calm, yes?'
he added as he put out a hand and opened the door.

Leonie's first impression was of a large, white-walled
and airy room, two sides of which were composed of
arches open to a wide verandah overlooking the far
mountain peaks. Trembling nervously in the doorway,
her eyes were irresistibly drawn past the two nurses
present towards the small, frail figure of the girl lying
on a narrow bed in the centre of the room.

Why—she's no more than a child! Leonie thought,
swept by a tide of deep pity and compassion as the
doctor led her over to a chair beside the bed. It was all
she could do not to cry out in distress as she found

herself staring down at the pitifully gaunt, stick-thin frame of a young girl. Her face, surrounded by long black hair, was deathly pale, only the brilliant dark eyes burned fiercely, glowing feverishly as they surveyed the woman bending over her.

'You . . . you are Leonie?' Aisha murmured, her thin lips curving into a sweet smile. 'I hope . . . I understand you speak Arabic?'

'Yes,' Leonie whispered nervously, lowering herself down on the chair and trying not to show how shocked she was at the sight of the other girl's wasted limbs.

'That is good—my English is very, very bad!' She lapsed into Arabic, once again giving Leonie a sweet smile, her thin chest heaving as she fought for breath. 'I wanted to see you . . . it is very important that I tell you . . . tell you . . .'

'Please! Please don't try to speak too much,' Leonie murmured, her tender heart going out to the frail girl whose laboured breathing was a heart-wrenching sight. Without thinking she took Aisha's thin fingers into her own warm hand. 'Surely you should rest and conserve your strength?' she added.

'No. No, I have no time!' Aisha rasped. 'And I know . . . I know that it is so important I tell you that Badyr and I . . .' She began to cough, a nurse swiftly materialising by her side to gently sponge the perspiration from the Arab girl's face.

'Poor Badyr, he has been burdened with me for so long. Never has he shown the least impatience . . .' She paused to catch her breath. 'Because of his great kindness, and because he is so unhappy and desolate, I knew I must tell you . . .' She faltered, looking up at the girl beside her. 'Yes,' she sighed. 'Yes, you are as lovely, as beautiful as Badyr always said you were.' She gave another heavy sigh. 'I must confess I was always jealous of you. So silly of me, hmm?' Aisha gave a small, wry smile.

'And I of you,' Leonie whispered, tears filling her

eyes as a hard lump of pity and sorrow obstructed her throat.

'Of—*of me?* How foolish of you!' The girl gave a rasping, incredulous laugh which shook her frail figure. 'That is why I wanted to see you. Why I had to tell you that Badyr and I have never . . . never lived together. Not . . . not as man and wife, you understand?' she panted. 'I knew that it . . . it was important that I tell you this, yes?'

'Oh, Aisha!' Leonie grabbed some tissues from a box beside the bed, fiercely blowing her nose and wiping the tears from her eyes.

'Poor Badyr. He has loved you so long . . . and so well. He was always so kind to me . . . but he could not bring himself to touch me . . . could not act that which was not in his heart . . .'

The girl's voice died away as she lay back on the pillows and closed her eyes, clearly exhausted by the effort of speaking so much. 'Yes . . .' she murmured, her breathless voice breaking into the long silence at last. 'Yes, it is true that I love him. I, too, love Badyr with all my heart—even a poor creature such as I! Alas, I can give him nothing.' A sob rasped in her throat. 'But I thought that if you knew the truth, Leonie . . .?' The thin talons of her hand gripped that of the English girl, agitatedly trying to raise her thin, wasted body. 'He says little, but I know you are estranged because of my marriage to him. He is so unhappy. Can you not forgive him? His marriage to me was not . . . not of his making. Surely you can understand—and learn to love him again?'

Tears were streaming down Leonie's cheeks, her figure shaking with sobs as she realised the depth of Aisha's unselfish, hopeless love for Badyr.

'Please, do not cry.' The breath rasped in Aisha's throat. 'All I ask of you is that you do not throw away his love and devotion. It is so very . . . very rare, is it not?'

'I promise you that I never stopped loving Badyr,' Leonie whispered. 'I tried, but I found that I couldn't,' she faltered, swept by a devastating sense of shame. 'He tried to tell me the truth, but I wouldn't listen!' she cried. 'It's all my fault!'

'Oh, no! I too am married to Badyr. I also know him well, you understand? I think he was frightened.'

'Badyr—frightened?' Leonie gazed incredulously at the girl through her tears.

'Oh, yes!' Aisha's lips curved into a wry smile. 'Even Badyr is human! He feared to lose you for ever. And when you discovered our marriage . . . how silly of him not to tell you the truth! . . . and you would not listen to him . . . he became too proud to beg . . . to confess to you why he married me. Yes, I love him, Leonie. But loving brings knowledge of weakness, as well as strength. So, I know he is kind and good . . . but he can also be stubborn and arrogant. Oh yes!'

The two girls found themselves grinning warmly at each other through their tears.

'So, you see? We are friends, yes?' Aisha whispered, smiling up at Leonie.

'Yes,' Leonie nodded, sniffing as she wiped away her tears. 'It is so generous of you to tell me everything. Is there anything you need, anything I can do for you?'

'No, I am just happy that we have met and talked,' Aisha murmured, her breathing becoming less laboured as if eased by being able to tell Leonie at last all that had been on her mind for so long. 'I can see that you will soon be having a baby, hmm?' she added. 'And Badyr says you have a little daughter, whom he loves very much. Please tell me all about her.'

Leonie felt almost too choked with emotion to comply with the girl's request. 'Well, her name is Jade and she was five years old last April,' Leonie began, holding Aisha's hand as the girl lay peacefully back on the pillows and closed her eyes. 'She is very like her father, possessing both his temper and the same

determination to get her own way!' Encouraged by
Aisha's grunt of laughter, she went on to describe
Jade's love of hopelessly unsuitable words, and her
current craze for learning to ride. 'Of course, her great-
uncle Feisal—who is her great hero—spoils her
outrageously,' she was saying as she became aware of
the doctor standing beside her.

Looking up, she saw him lean over the prone figure
of the girl on the bed, staring at him in bewilderment as
he gently removed her hand from Aisha's and slowly
drew the sheet up over the Arab girl's pale face.

'No! Oh no!' she cried, swept by a feeling of utter
desolation. 'Oh no ... please say it isn't true,' she
begged helplessly, slumping back in the chair and
burying her face in her hands.

'Ah, Majesty,' the doctor murmured, putting an arm
about her shoulders and helping her trembling figure to
rise. 'You must not weep for the Sultana Aisha. It was
only her determination to see you which had kept her
alive so long. She is surely now at peace, safe and well
in Allah's loving arms.'

'But we had only just become friends, and ... and
there was so much I wanted to say—so many things I'll
never be able to tell her!' Leonie sobbed as he led her
slowly towards the door.

'Death is not to be feared. It is merely a door
leading into a new world for the Sultana. One in
which she has already cast aside the frail, sick frame
with which she was forced to inhabit this life. Her
true purity of soul is now shining whole and beautiful
among the blessed,' he said softly. 'You must not
begrudge her the happiness of which she is now most
surely possessed, nor fear that she does not see and
know all that is in your heart.'

Leonie, the tears streaming down her face, allowed
herself to be led from the room and back down the
corridor. Almost paralysed with grief, she was hardly
aware of being helped into the waiting limousine, and

was still sobbing helplessly when the vehicle arrived back at the palace. Trembling with anguish and remorse, she stumbled from the car—and into her husband's arms.

'Oh, Badyr!' she wailed. 'Poor Aisha—she's ... she's ...'

'Yes. Yes, I know, my darling,' he murmured, holding her closely and gently stroking her hair.

'I've been so stupid! So blind and cruel! And ... and I love you with all my heart,' she sobbed. 'How can you ever forgive me?'

'There is nothing to forgive—unless we must beg forgiveness of each other,' Badyr said quietly. 'By her generosity of spirit, Aisha has given us both the chance of a new life together. Can we not accept and treasure such a precious gift, hmm?'

Raising her tear-stained face to his, Leonie became aware that Badyr was standing very still, a muscle beating wildly in his jaw as he waited for her answer.

'Oh, yes—yes, please,' she whispered, feeling the breath being slowly expelled from his powerful body in a long-drawn-out, emotional sigh before he crushed her passionately in his arms, his mouth covering her trembling lips in a kiss of fierce, hungry possession.

Later that evening, Leonie awoke from a sleep of deep exhaustion, which had claimed her tired mind and body almost from the minute that Badyr, having carried her upstairs, had laid her on their soft bed. Turning her head, she saw his tall, lithe figure rise from an easy chair as he moved over to sit down beside her.

'You are feeling better now, my love?' he asked anxiously.

'Yes, I ...' She faltered as he gently helped her to sit up against the pillows. 'We must talk. I hardly know how to begin to apologise ...'

'What need is there for apologies between us, my darling?' he said softly, as his arms closed gently about her. 'I fell hopelessly and quite irresistibly in love with you—an adorable, innocent and shy young girl—when you called at my apartment all those years ago. From that moment, absolutely nothing has changed the deep emotional feelings I have for you, my beloved.'

Leonie stared down at her quivering hands, before forcing herself to meet Badyr's intense gaze. 'I never stopped loving you, either,' she murmured softly. 'I . . . I did try, but . . .' She sighed helplessly as she leant back against the pillows. 'I know that I've been incredibly stupid at times, but we've had such a very complicated married life, Badyr. Please don't blame me too much for . . . well, for doubting your feelings for me.'

'How could I ever blame you for anything!' he said huskily, taking her trembling figure into his arms. 'So much has been my fault. Right from the first. From the moment we married, our love was put under such an intolerable strain.' He sighed deeply. 'I should have waited. I should have had enough self-control to wait until after the coup against my father before marrying you. But I wanted you so much, my darling! You were so very young, like a rose in bud, perfect and unawakened, and I feared that some other man would steal you from me while I was away. I nearly became demented at the thought of an unknown stranger teaching you the delights of physical love, receiving your first shy responses and hearing those sweet cries of rapture,' he groaned, buring his face in the soft cleft of her breasts.

'I . . . er . . . I did beg you to marry me and take me to Dhoman,' she murmured, gently running her fingers through his black hair.

'Yes, but I should have been sensible enough to know what a disaster it would turn out to be. But where you are concerned, my darling, I am as weak as water.' He raised his head to give her a lingering kiss. 'The only excuse I can offer is that I had been away from this country for so long, that I did not realise the full extent of either my father's despotic rule or his unstable temperament.'

'The poor man,' Leonie mused. 'I feel sorry for him. I realise now that he just couldn't cope with life in the twentieth century.'

Badyr turned to lie on his back, staring up at the ceiling. 'You are more generous than I,' he sighed. 'It is a sin to conspire against one's father, and I shall have to answer for my actions at the day of judgment—of that there is no doubt. But when I used your sweetness to assuage my anger and frustration against my father ... it was right that I should have reaped a full punishment for such cruelty. And I was punished, Leonie,' he added in a low, throbbing voice. 'I do not think that there was one hour, of those five, seemingly endless years, when I did not yearn for your sweet presence.'

'Aisha?' she whispered tremulously.

For a moment there was silence, and then Badyr rolled over to gather her gently into his arms. 'The Americans have an expression: "over a barrel", and that is just what I was—well and truly over a barrel—when I heard how my father was threatening you. I was so ... so damned *helpless*! If I wished to make sure you were safe, I had no alternative but to marry a girl I had never seen in my life. I have learnt to forgive my mother, who only did what she felt was in the interests of the country; but when I took that dreadful decision, every one of us suffered as a consequence. The poor, frail little girl,' he added softly. 'Aisha was so frightened when she arrived down at the Summer Palace. Can you imagine how terrified she must have been? She had no mother, and her father had just been arrested. She had never

travelled more than a few miles from her home in the
north of the country, and when she quickly became
so ill ...' He sighed deeply. 'I knew that I was
responsible, Leonie. I had chosen to save you, but in
doing so I had unwittingly condemned her. Can you
understand?'

'Of course I do,' she murmured, tenderly pressing
her lips to the strained lines about his mouth. 'I'm
only ashamed that ... that when I discovered her
existence, I didn't give you a chance to tell me the
truth.'

He hesitated. 'From the beginning I had told her how
I felt about you, and that it was not possible ... that
our marriage must be in name only.'

'I know. Aisha told me. Oh, Badyr! If only I could
have met her sooner. And now it's too late,' she
whispered, hiding her face in the warm curve of his
shoulder.

'Aisha was a sweet, generous girl of whom I became
very fond, and for whom I cared deeply—but she was
not you, my darling,' he said simply, his lips kissing
away the tears from her eyes.

Some minutes later, Badyr slowly and reluctantly
let her go. 'I think I am going to break one of my
golden rules,' he said huskily as he got up off the
bed. 'Attempting to keep myself away from you has
been a damned torture—I've never had so many
freezing cold showers in my whole life as I've been
having these last few weeks! So, I suggest we have
some champagne on ice, which may help to cool my
ardour.'

Leonie couldn't help smiling through her tears at his
rueful expression. 'Don't you laugh at me, you witch!'
he muttered in mock fury, picking up the internal
phone and issuing an order. 'Which reminds me,' he
added, 'I must have an urgent word with the worthy
Dr Winslow. I can see that it might be dangerous at
the moment, but when you've given birth to the baby,

just how many hellish weeks will I have to endure
before I can make love to you?'

'It's no good looking at me for the answer!' she
retorted, smiling as his tall figure paced about the
room. 'I'll have you know that I led a thoroughly pure
life after Jade was born!'

'*Wallahi!* I can't begin to tell you how I worried
about *that* fact!' he growled. 'I kept as close an eye on
your life in London as I could, but I can assure you that
I went through the tortures of the damned, worrying
incessantly about your relationships with other men! As
soon as I took over the rule of this country from my
father, I realised that if I'd been over a barrel before, it
was nothing to the situation in which I found myself
then. I was damned certain that you'd *never* accept the
fact of my second marriage. I know,' he said over her
muttered protest. 'You might have been understanding, but it was a hell of a risk for me to take, all the
same. On the other hand, I simply couldn't bring
myself to divorce Aisha—it would have been far too
cruel to treat her in such a way.' He sighed. 'I give
you my solemn word that I have never, ever, wished
for her death. I realised that I must simply bury
myself in the necessary work involved in pulling
Dhoman into the twentieth century, and let fate
decide what was to happen.'

He paused as there was a knock at the door, and
Hussa entered with a tray. Putting it down on a small
table, she winked at Leonie and scurried out of the
room.

'Hussa is clearly an incurable romantic!' Badyr
laughed wryly as he placed a cold glass of bubbling
champagne in his wife's hand. 'She never ceased to
ask after you, urging me to bring you back to
Dhoman. Of course, I shouldn't have taken the risk,
but when I received your mother's letter telling me
about her marriage, and just how worried she was
about you—I decided to take the gamble. I now see

that it was incredibly foolish of me, but although I am a patient man, I knew that I could no longer endure life without you by my side. And as soon as we kissed, that first time we met again in the Embassy, I *knew* you still cared for me! That unless something went badly wrong—which, of course, it did—I had taken the right decision. However, being certain that you still felt something for me, was one matter. Trying to handle an extremely difficult, temperamental and obstinate wife—was quite another! Getting you back to Dhoman was one of the most difficult tasks I've ever attempted. It was like trying to woo a cage full of rattlesnakes!'

'Charming! And what's this nonsense about trying to "woo" me?' Leonie gave a sardonic laugh. 'There was nothing lover-like about you—you horrible man! The sound of a door-bell still makes me shudder, and as for that fur coat . . .!'

'Ah, beloved. You looked so beautiful, so ravishingly lovely, that I nearly raped you there and then in the zoo!' He laughed at the bright crimson flush spreading across her cheeks.

'Yes, well . . . I suppose I was in a bit of a state,' she admitted. 'And although I like to think I would have been understanding, if you'd told me about Aisha when you came to London, I don't know . . . I can't honestly say what my reaction would have been.'

Badyr stared sadly down at his glass. 'I want to tell you that those long months, when you insisted on being left alone at the Summer Palace, were a far worse torture than the five years' absence between us. No, I never believed for a moment that you would seek to lose the baby you carried,' he assured her. 'But, not a day went by, when I didn't decide to fly down and *make* you listen to the truth. But always I stopped before doing so. I knew that I was responsible for your deep hurt and anger, but I also—

alas—became angry and stiff with pride. I told myself that if you had loved me, you would have made some effort to understand, and I ... I could not bring myself to make the necessary explanations, a gesture which I foolishly saw as a crawling humiliation.'

'Oh, Badyr ...' Her eyes filled with tears. 'I've caused you—both of us—so much pain!'

'Enough!' he commanded firmly. 'We have both been unhappy long enough, hmm? Sweet, kind Aisha has given us the chance to renew our marriage—a legacy that we must treasure. Not only do we have a lovely and amusing daughter, but we will soon be blessed with another child. With so much for which to be thankful, my darling, let us now look forward to the happy future—not backwards to the mistakes we have made in the past,' he added huskily, his mouth possessing hers in a pledge of warmth and tenderness.

Four months later Leonie sat gazing idly out of the window at the fiery sun slipping slowly down over the horizon. They had been at the Summer Palace for almost a week, and already she had slipped under its lazy, carefree spell. In the distance she could hear the fishermen calling to each other as they left their boats, while nearer at hand Jade was laughing as her father told her a good-night story.

Sighing with contentment, Leonie lowered her head to smile at the baby in her arms. With fluffy, jet-black hair, Karim was the very image of Badyr, the only legacy from his mother being the startling, sapphire-blue eyes hidden now by his drowsy eyelids, as he lay sleepily content and replete at her breast.

'I would find it very easy to become jealous of my son and heir!' a voice said softly. Smiling up at Badyr's tall figure as he walked across the floor of the nursery, she instinctively attempted to cover herself. 'Ah, no, my beloved. Do not hide your loveliness from me,' he murmured, sitting down beside her and gently tracing a path with his fingers over the burgeoning fulness of her bare breasts.

'Your son is greedy—just like his father!' she grinned, wiping a small trickle of milk from the baby's chin. Although she spoke lightly, her nerve-ends tingled and throbbed at his intimate touch. Karim's birth had not been an easy one, and she was aware of just how inhibiting Badyr had found that fact, striving to carefully restrain his ardour when they had resumed their lovemaking. But she was already feeling a great deal stronger, her body becoming eager and impatient to welcome the full force of his passion.

'Ah,' Badyr sighed, regretfully moving his hand as Leonie lifted the baby to her shoulder, gently patting his back. 'Before I become too carried away, I must tell you three pieces of interesting news. First, I have had a reply to my cable, and you will be pleased to hear that your mother and stepfather will be joining us here in a week's time.'

'I'm so glad they can make it—it will be lovely to see my mother again,' she smiled happily.

'And for her to see her new grandchild, hmm?' He gently stroked his son's cheek. 'Karim is a very clever child—did I tell you that he smiled at me today?' Badyr added proudly.

'That was probably wind!' she teased. 'What are the other two bits of news?'

'Well, you may ... er ... remember that I was paralytically angry with that wretched sister of mine, Nadia. In my fury, I sent her off to some cousins in Saudi Arabia. They belong to a very strict religious sect and I thought that life with them might give her something to think about,' he added grimly. 'However, to my utter amazement, I received a letter today from the head of the family, telling me that Nadia has fallen madly in love with an elderly prince, and is requesting my permission to marry him.' A slow smile spread across Badyr's face. 'The cream of the jest is that he already has two wives and countless children! I have, of course, despatched my sincere congratulations—and a huge dowry, just in case the poor man should think of changing his mind!'

'That's really rotten of you!' Leonie tried not to laugh. 'Even Nadia doesn't deserve to get herself into that sort of mess. She's bound to be unhappy before very long.'

'No—I think not. Nadia is the child most like my father. I will wager you any sum you care to mention, that she will quickly manage to persuade her husband to cast aside his two other wives, disinheriting his children in favour of any she may have—and then proceed to make his life a misery. Believe me—the poor man will need all the consolation of a large dowry!' he laughed. 'And talking of weddings: I was approached today by my uncle Feisal. I must confess to being somewhat embarrassed that a man, so much older than I, should feel the need to ask my permission to get married.'

Leonie gasped. 'Not . . .?'

'Yes, he wishes to marry our governess! I have already had a word with Elizabeth, and she tells me that—always provided that Feisal faithfully promises not to bring his horses into their house, or to take a second wife—she thinks she might like to marry a *real* Sheikh of Araby!'

'Goodness—how exciting!' she laughed. 'I must go and have a word with her right away.'

'No—not just at the moment,' Badyr murmured, taking the sleeping baby from her arms and placing him in his cot. 'Having attended to the needs of my son, I think it is time you turned your full attention to the requirements of his father, don't you?' he added as he led her through into their bedroom, firmly closing the door before taking her into his arms.

Laughter gleamed in the depths of her blue eyes.

'Darling, Badyr,' she whispered as she became aware of the passion throbbing in his body, and the rising tide of desire beginning to sweep through her veins. 'How could I possibly presume to disagree with my husband? I wouldn't dare to be guilty of such ... such *lèse-majesté!*'

Harlequin Presents

Coming Next Month

Available in January wherever paperback books are sold, or through Harlequin Reader Service:

In the U.S.
P.O. Box 1397
Buffalo, N.Y.
14240-1397

In Canada
P.O. Box 603
Fort Erie, Ontario
L2A 9Z9

Can you keep a secret?

You can keep this one plus 4 free novels

Six exciting series for you every month... from Harlequin

Harlequin Romance·
The series that started it all

Tender, captivating and heartwarming...
love stories that sweep you off to faraway places
and delight you with the magic of love.

◆

Harlequin Presents·
Powerful contemporary love stories...as individual as the women who read them

The No. 1 romance series...
exciting love stories for you, the woman of today...
a rare blend of passion and dramatic realism.

◆

Harlequin Superromance®
It's more than romance... it's Harlequin Superromance

A sophisticated, contemporary romance-fiction
series, providing you with a longer,
more involving read...a richer mix of complex plots,
realism and adventure.

Harlequin
American Romance™
Harlequin celebrates the American woman...

...by offering you romance stories written about American women, by American women for American women. This series offers you contemporary romances uniquely North American in flavor and appeal.

◆

Harlequin Temptation™
Passionate stories for today's woman

An exciting series of sensual, mature stories of love...dilemmas, choices, resolutions... all contemporary issues dealt with in a true-to-life fashion by some of your favorite authors.

◆

Harlequin Intrigue
Because romance can be quite an adventure

Harlequin Intrigue, an innovative series that blends the romance you expect... with the unexpected. Each story has an added element of intrigue that provides a new twist to the Harlequin tradition of romance excellence.

Harlequin Books·

PROD-A-2

Janet Dailey
Americana

Don't miss a single title from this great collection. The first eight titles have already been published. Complete and mail this coupon today to order books you may have missed.

Harlequin Reader Service

In U.S.A.
901 Fuhrmann Blvd.
P.O. Box 1397
Buffalo, N.Y. 14140

In Canada
P.O. Box 2800
Postal Station A
5170 Yonge Street
Willowdale, Ont. M2N 6J3

Please send me the following titles from the Janet Dailey Americana Collection. I am enclosing a check or money order for $2.75 for each book ordered, plus 75¢ for postage and handling.

_____	ALABAMA	Dangerous Masquerade
_____	ALASKA	Northern Magic
_____	ARIZONA	Sonora Sundown
_____	ARKANSAS	Valley of the Vapours
_____	CALIFORNIA	Fire and Ice
_____	COLORADO	After the Storm
_____	CONNECTICUT	Difficult Decision
_____	DELAWARE	The Matchmakers

Number of titles checked @ $2.75 each = $_____

N.Y. RESIDENTS ADD
    APPROPRIATE SALES TAX $_____

Postage and Handling $____.75____

                                      TOTAL $_____

I enclose _____

(Please send check or money order. We cannot be responsible for cash sent through the mail.)

PLEASE PRINT

NAME _____

ADDRESS _____

CITY _____

STATE/PROV. _____

BLJD-A-1